PROCLAMATIONS

Except for an early morning spider that crawled into my scotch; no animals were harmed during the writing of this novel.

This is a work of fiction. Any human finding a resemblance to themselves needs help. Badly needs help. Get thee to a sanatorium. Now!

This novel is not for everyone. It's scary, irreverent, modestly profane, and thought provoking. Or something.

To the readers who love this book: May all your children be beautiful, your pockets lined with gold, and your sex life rival Satan's.

To the readers who dislike this book: Let the author recommend the writings of... Oh, never mind. You wouldn't like them either.

Women are God's best effort thus far. Men are, well... they're men. The author is sorry.

EVERYONE: Give to your local Humane Society. Yes, this author does.

SÉANCE & SAUCER

BY

ROBERT RIFE

FOR MY DAUGHTER

Deep Portal Publishing
Polydactyl Productions
Seattle, Washington (USA)

SÉANCE & SAUCER

ISBN: 979-8-9862806-5-3 (Paperback)
       979-8-9862806-6-0 (Hardcover)
       979-8-9862806-7-7 (eBook)

Editing: Victoria Edwards
Cover design: Arcane Books
Interior Design by Booknook.biz.

SÉANCE & SAUCER

PROLOGUE

It is an immense idol—a colossal rock, towering over him. The man scoffs at this cheap conjuring trick.

Its mouth opens.

He turns to run.

Slow is not a survival skill.

CHAPTER 1

WRAITHS TODAY, HELL TOMORROW

The two-story, vine cloaked Roaton house was bad at birth. Deeply wrong. Dark and ominous is not an adequate description. It broods.

When construction started, it was already damned. From the murdered-for land, to the tribe-sacred timber stolen, the Victorian structure was cursed.

And it took people. It kept them. They were seen now and then... peering from the dark windows.

As decades passed, ownership of the property changed a few times. But only on tax documents, never in reality. No one owned the Roaton Place. The house did the owning.

This house also has a physical connection far beyond any curse. In its basement is a door that should not exist. It opens into a long-buried starship. Centuries old... but not quiet. Not dead.

This dwelling holds many surprises.

Most are fatal.

Some are worse. A lot worse than death.

And the Roaton house is patient. It simply waits for someone it wants. Through its long years of existence, it has rarely been bored.

Nor will it be today.

———◆◆◆———

RL, the current fool who thinks he owns the Roaton place, climbs the curved staircase. Checking the ironed creases in his jeans, being sure the blue chambray shirt is tucked properly and sleeves cuffed evenly. He notes the shine on his loafers and so on. All this is capped off with some strategic raking of fingers through medium short, graying hair. He does this several times and it still looks like a stunted tumbleweed.

This is preening. RL would never call it that. But everyone else does.

He's also concocting money-making schemes along with the lies to make them palatable. He's always doing this, and he's good at it. He has to be. He deals in antiques, where over-pricing and agility with truth are professional requirements.

Halfway up the stairs all thoughts of preening, money... and breathing, are wrenched from him.

Fear replaces them. Sweat beads his face, seeping into that blue shirt, showing dark at the collar.

On the second-floor landing hovers a pulsing cloud of vapor, formed from twisting coils of mist. Three strands of curling malevolence dart from it like tongues, then slide back into the writhing mass. Cold spills down the steps toward him; the bitter chill of things that have not finished dying.

RL knows these things; he knows these apparitions.

They had attacked him on these same stairs not long ago. But he'd believed them gone, banished by something even they feared. And he'd been totally sure they would never be seen again. Or he wouldn't be here now.

Not to show panic, which might make them attack, he slowly backs down. Only taking one step at a time, revealing no fear, no hurry. Close to the bottom, he casually turns. If he could, he would whistle gaily. But right now, dust would come out.

Then RL's true and brave nature takes over.

He runs like a rabbit on fire. He runs with bulging eyes, ballooning bladder and dignity abandoned.

Yes, RL remembers the wraiths very well.

Below him, a door flies open, crashing against a wall, sending echoes bouncing through this tomb of a house.

Out from that opened door boils a gray hued, swirling embodiment of feminine wrath. Not even specters can match a woman's rage. Just ask a cheating husband.

RL hits the ground floor in a coward's sprint, sees the woman, and shrieks manfully at her.

"YOUR DAUGHTERS ARE BACK!"

The shit has hit. Officially.

If any human could truly claim ownership of the Roaton House, it was this gray person. Except she was not human. Not exactly. Not precisely.

No one knew what she was, including the woman herself... because she *was* the house. When decades of a brutal husband had driven her mad, the house had taken her. Absorbed her. Knitted her into its fabric.

The house got more than it wanted. The woman also took the house. They both eventually accepted this. And each gained from it. Prospective owners did not gain. They usually left at the sight of her. In great haste.

———•◆•———

At this same time, a few miles away, a silly bastard fusses with merchandise and giggles to himself.

Frankie also admires his reflection in the shop's freestanding mirror; the same mirror he grotesquely over-prices to customers. So grotesquely, they could buy one at the Louvre for less. He loves this mirror. Particularly its reflection.

Frankie believes appearance is always important. And absolutely necessary when preparing to cheat all hell out of someone. His chartreuse ensemble looks lovely, he's quite sure. A very light chartreuse... with matching belt and loafers.

Yes, lovely indeed. This is preening. And that's exactly what Frankie calls it. RL, his business partner, uses other words to describe this fluttering about.

He smooths his pants over a small bulge. The bulge is a Prod, a trinket stolen from a buried UFO. Its settings range from sending an intense *itch,* to *sizzling, bubbling roast.* The latter adjustment kills really well. Frankie considers it a dandy pocket tool, especially for customers who won't buy. He giggles at the thought.

Taking a loving look at the halogen-lighted jewelry case next to the register, he feels the display is an absolute work of art and genius. Frankie being the genius.

Plucking a small bronze statue from the display's top, he replaces it with an intricately carved walking stick, leaning it against the register. A much better attention puller than the bronze. And the cane looks old enough to have been used by Moses while he was playing around in the desert.

It had been carved in Jakarta about three weeks ago.

Some judicious sanding and staining had aged the stick a bit... but only by a few centuries. Mustn't get too carried away when creating an antique. Someone might get suspicious of the other crap they've bought here.

There were six more canes in the back, each to be displayed one at a time. Belief in rarity is much easier to achieve when antiquities are rationed.

The shop door reads: NEAT STUFF, and now chimes as it opens. Announcing money. An absolutely magical sound.

Frankie's face blossoms into an open smile, perfectly framing his chipped front tooth. His cowlick wags with innocent charm. A grown Boy Scout. Honest. True. Morally straight.

Oh yes. Absolutely straight and honest. He's so full of ethics he stays constipated.

And everything here is guaranteed. Guaranteed to be older than yesterday. Maybe even older than last week. Just ask Frankie, who wouldn't tell a lie. Unless really, really necessary.

Frankie is also guaranteed... to be full of something.

The customer is a tiny old woman with a purse big enough to house livestock. Along with their hay. Outside glitters a new Mercedes.

Frankie's spirit soars. Fresh fleecing is on the way. He's already counting the money. Hers, and a ton of it.

He's lethal with women. Especially elderly ones. It's that Boy Scout shit.

And this old dear, clutching that purse to her withered bosom, has treasure written all over her. She might as well have gutted herself before entering, and save Frankie the effort.

Beaming his apple-pie wholesomeness, he approaches. How sweet and grandmotherly she is. How dear, how kind. How wonderfully gullible. The poor silly old fool.

And her tender, aged lips speak:

"I bet you're the faggot cock-sucker that cheated my daughter! If you ain't, then go get your partner's ass out here," the sweet old woman says, producing a huge pistol from the purse.

Frankie's smile collapses.

The cowlick droops.

...Well, penetrate me with a hammer. Granny Good just turned into Ma Barker.

Frankie's day is not starting well.

It's about to get a lot worse.

—◆◆◆—

Back at the Roaton house, the gray woman only nods, acknowledging RL's shrieked warning about her daughters.

"Yes," she says softly, already moving toward the staircase. "I sensed their foulness moments ago as they entered my home. They are why I have come. Why I left my room."

She is a charcoal portrait given motion. No color, no pigment, only shades of black and gray, with alabaster scars and knots where bones have not knitted properly. A woman like storm water, long beaten against cliffs.

Except for her eyes.

Her eyes have color... sometimes.

"Shadow, I, I, I saw you drive them away before! How can they be back?" squeaks RL.

Ignoring him, she reaches the foot of the stairs. She massages her badly healed arms, kneading at old breaks with black finger nails. Her gaze climbs the steps to the pulsing mass of light and movement above. The ebony lips pull back from her teeth.

When she speaks, her voice sounds like stones thrown into a crypt. Stones *ordered* into a crypt. And eager to get in where it's safe; away from her.

"I WILL NOT ABIDE YOU HERE! None of you are what once was, nor can you ever be. Return to that which you now embrace. Go."

The cloud convulses, pulsating anger.

It swells outward like a lung drawing breath. Its center tears open into a spinning vortex of a mouth; a dead cave lined with unholy light.

Three wraiths leap from it, coiling and striking, their twisted faces silently screaming.

———— ✦ ————

Back in the city, having a granny pull a cannon out of her purse and call him a cheating faggot, is not an entirely new thing for Frankie. He does deal in antiques, and this is Texas. A state where citizens are known to occasionally police citizens. It's often needed.

And Frankie would proudly, gleefully, *eagerly* say, that yes, he *is* a faggot. He's as gay as a butt plug. He'd say it with absolute relish. As to the cheating... well, it all depends on which part of a deal is being examined. And who's doing the looking.

Eyeing granny and her gun, Frankie goes into a Frankie act:

"Oh, my goodness!" he wails. (clapping his hands to both cheeks)

"Oh, my! No!" he bleats. (going pigeon toed)

"I could never ever, ever cheat anyone!" he whines. (wrapping both arms around his chest)

Before Frankie can get to the crying part of this act, the sweet, benevolent Gran-Gran cuts in.

"If you keep flappin' them pecker-tongs around, I'm gonna put some lead in your liver. You just keep them hands still, and don't raise'em over your head neither. I don't want no attention from the laws."

Frankie sighs, letting the act die, and dropping his hands. The gun's bore looks cavernous. Seriously big.

Imminent death is always serious.

"You listen up, Whistle Britches," continues sweet granny. "I wasn't born in that Mercedes with a silver spoon stickin' outta my ass. Until they hit oil, I growed up hard, so this six-shooter ain't for show."

Oh, shit... the old bat is Oil Money... donates big time locally, figures she can get away with anything. But if I can just get that Prod out...

"Ma'am," Frankie says, carefully smiling again, "this must be a slight misunderstanding. Please tell me what this alleged cheating is ab—"

"Ain't no *alleged* to it, Queenie. Them diamonds is mine," she says pointing at the jewelry case.

"My druggie daughter stole that there necklace outta my joolry box. And you can bet your sweet ass she won't thieve from me no more."

Frankie shuts down the smile. The bore of that gun is looking bigger. Big enough to hold a grave. His grave.

"Well, ma'am, I'm ever so sure she will never steal from you again," he says in a neutral tone.

The old woman ignores this, looking back and forth between him and the necklace. And holding the pistol very steady... on Frankie. Then the elderly dear speaks.

"And I'll just lay odds that you got a boner when you first seen that neckwear of mine."

Granny is correct. Frankie had indeed been... aroused when he'd seen the sparkler, but he feels now is not the time to admit this. No, now is the time for maneuverings. Careful maneuverings.

Frankie tries again.

"Ma'am! Please, there's no need for such crudity. Many pieces of jewelry look much the same when viewed alongside—"

"Shut it, Flat Knees. We ain't goin' there. I know them diamonds, and they're mine. I mean to take'em."

Frankie has no intention of letting this damned crone leave with her own property. The very idea! There is no profit in honesty.

"Well, ma'am," Frankie says, edging a hand toward the Prod in his pocket. "If you'll just let me—"

"I see that hand twitchin', boy," she snaps. "You're tryin' my patience," she continues, cocking the pistol. It is a very loud sound.

"Okay, okay! You win, ma'am. I'll get you the necklace."

She laughs, sounding like a donkey choking.

"Oh, Sweet Cheeks, you're a one, ain't you! You likely got a pantywaist automatic hid back there. You just rest easy and I'll get it myself."

Heaving a theatrical sigh, Frankie simply says, "Fine. The keys are just beneath the register, under some dust cloths."

Moving behind the counter, revolver steady, she notices the cane. The cane that Moses had carried.

"That's a sin-purty old walkin' stick. I just might take that too, seein' as how I been to so much trouble on account of you."

Bending to look under the register, she continues.

"Yep, sure enough, there's a little bitty pop-pistol back here. Hell, I bet sometimes you hide that up your crack, and just get all worked up over—"

Frankie moves with the speed of a whore taking money. Grabbing the cane, he clubs the shit out of that dear precious old head.

Her gun fires.

———— ✦✦ ————

Back at the Roaton house, the open maw from that pulsing cloud lunges down at Shadow. Like snakes, three wraiths from within strike out at the gray woman, their faces blazing with silent fury.

Shadow does not step back, does not flinch, does not blink.

Decades ago, when she was called Anna, she'd borne these three. She has seen far worse than death and ghosts since. To her, they are but dim visions straining for release through the past's veil.

She is the house now. She no longer fears the other side. Or fears any side.

But RL certainly does. He stands frozen, beyond fear... he's truly terrified. These things had once viciously battered his friend into a coma, and nearly gotten him. Only Shadow's arrival had saved them. It's not something he's likely to forget.

The wraiths, these once-daughters, recoil and strike down, again and again. Never hitting, but darting and rippling around her face in frustration.

Shadow laughs, but it is a tired, mirthless sound.

"Throw your tantrums, you dreary little wisps of nothing. You cannot touch me. Nor will I permit you to harm anyone in my presence. I do not know how you met your end, but you *chose* this existence at death. I am sorry for you. And sorry that I could not protect you from your father, that utter beast I was forced to wed."

She looks at the lunging, darting faces a few seconds, shaking her head with finality.

"But you tried to murder my Elv-is. For that, there will be no forgiveness. Thank whatever god you have chosen, that I do not come after you. Go now. Weep your bitterness."

The writhing knot of horror vanishes, like the flipping of a switch.

RL collapses to his knees, shirt soaked with sweat. He's grateful his jeans aren't soaked with something else.

"Christ Almighty, Shadow. Are they really gone?"

"No. They have not left the house. I do not think they will leave this time."

This is less than comforting news. Looking up at her, he slowly rises.

"But... but... can't you make them?"

"Yes," she answers, turning sharply to him. "By leaving what I am. By leaving the house. By dying."

Her jaws tighten, sparks of glowing white appearing in blue eyes.

"I will not leave Elv-is," she continues. "Not even to protect you and Jayderay, whom I also love." Her voice is becoming harsh. The eyes continue to whiten.

"We would never ask you to," RL says quickly, fearing her anger, the madness he's seen before.

"Shadow, we bought this place to save it from demolition, to keep it safe for you and Elvis. We owe you both our lives. But we *must* move in here, our finances demand it. So, how do we get rid of these... your... these ghost things?"

"I do not know," she says in a softer voice. "The house took me, not my daughters. They are dead, I am not. They are haunts, I am not." Glancing at her gray hands, she adds, "Regardless of my pallor." And gives him an almost smile, her eyes returning to normal.

"I'm sure Elvis doesn't object," says RL quickly, still wary of this volatile woman.

"No, most certainly not," she says, her smile becoming real. Like Mona Lisa's.

"Oh! I must return to him. He is weak, and they will be back!" She finishes that awful statement over her shoulder, leaving RL alone.

Alone and thinking hard about that "they will be back" part.

If they're still here in this house... then where in the house?

RL stares at the staircase, follows it up. His eyes widen.

... the attic... they're in the attic... of course they are... along with the monsters in the basement, and the bats in my brain... do we really HAVE to move here...

He hears whispers. Indistinct, slurred murmurs. Words from the dead.

Not from the attic.

They're coming out from the walls, up from the floor, down from the ceiling, out from everywhere. They hammer into him, leeching him.

Bravely dashing for the front door, RL decides the attic can wait.

Yes, the attic can wait. It can wait for Frankie.

As Frankie bashes the cane into sweet gran-gran's foul head, the dear old bitch squawks and shoots. Frankie screams.

Frantically examining his precious front for the hole he's sure his innards are pouring out of... he finds nothing. Not even powder burns.

He peers quickly over the counter at Granny to make sure she's not preparing for another try.

She's not. She's napping, as a purple lump rises through her thin white hair.

Frankie hopes it hurts.

"Well, Annie Oakly, seems you're not quite the hot shit shooter you thought you were."

Leaping behind the counter, he scoops up the revolver, stuffing it in his pants. Then racing to the shop door, locks it, and flips the sign to CLOSED.

Frankie hasn't survived a very interesting life by being slow or dim. He immediately starts planning on what to do with that unconscious body on the floor. (not a first for this shop) He's also wondering where that huge 45 caliber slug fired off to.

Frankie gasps with horror. Frankie grabs at his heart. Frankie starts sobbing.

"My mirror! The old bitch shot my mirror!" he wails, looking at the shattered remains. "Damn! And it *really* was an antique."

Storming to the counter, he glares down at the slayer of innocent mirrors.

She stirs feebly, moaning, waking.

Frankie yanks her pistol from his waist band, finger tightening on the trigger... but stops himself.

... No... better not... that would be going a teensy too far... and it would be messy... and RL would get all prissy and pouty about it. But damn it, she really does need killing... the greedy old trout.

Sighing wistfully, he reverses the gun, and with the butt, gently clubs granny again. She quits waking up. But starts snoring... loudly.

"Hell," he mutters aloud, "now I'm gonna have to listen to that racket. I swear, you just can't be considerate with some people. I might still shoot her."

The shop's land line rings. Phones always ring during the most inopportune times. It's a law. And they're inanimate, they enjoy this.

Glancing over, Frankie reads it's RL. Before answering, he speaks to Granny in a conspirator's tone.

"'Tis my lord and master, and with his usual bad timing. I've got to answer, or he'll think I'm up to something and drive over. So don't you get gabby, it might not be good for one of us."

"Hi, Boss, what's up?

"Plenty, and I need you out here to the Roaton place. Like 30 minutes ago," says the shaky sounding RL.

"Umm, uh… well, I've got a bit of a, uh, a teensy problem right now. But I've got it… in hand," he says glancing at the gun. And before he can stop himself, he giggles.

"God damn it, Frankie! You're up to something, but I don't have time to worm it out of you. Solve it, and get out here. They're back."

"Well… just *who* are they? The Clintons? Heckle and Jeckle? You know, I wouldn't mind seeing a Heckle and—"

"Oh, do shut up, Frankie. The ghosts are back!"

"Oh, shit!"

"I almost did. Shadow rescued me, but she said they won't leave and she can't make them."

"Well, if SHE can't, Mon Capitaine, what do you expect me to do?"

"You can give me courage to go back in there, for a start. Right now, I'm sitting in the van trying to get over my heart attack. So, take care of that 'teensy problem' you've no doubt caused, and get out here."

"RL, I'm totally innocent in this, really I am."

"You can't even spell that word. Now, get moving!" And RL disconnects.

These two business partners have the ethics of a toilet brush, and their morals can't be examined by the delicate. But they are loyal to each other.

And they do have good qualities, as they've both committed murder... in virtuous causes. The recipients really deserved killing. And needed it... this is Texas.

Frankie holds the dead phone, looking down at the twice smacked old woman. He must solve this, and get his silly ass moving.

... I didn't need your wretched, cantankerous ass to start my day with, and now it looks like you've set a pattern. It's going to be downhill for the rest of it... that's how shit flows.

Frankie empties her purse. And gets a bit of luck. Out bounces a big fat bottle of Oxys, without a prescription label. He wouldn't touch this poison for personal use, but he can use it to get out of his "teensy problem."

Frankie is getting up to something. He's known for this.

As he drags the trouble maker to the back of the shop, he says with great sincerity and feeling.

"You're gonna need that Oil Money influence to get out of this, old girl. And you needn't worry about that glittering fat rock you used to have on your finger. I'll take very good care of it."

Frankie will also give the same tender care to the roll of hundreds he liberated from the purse.

Dumping her at the back door, he listens for her continued snoring, then races to the front. Diving into the Mercedes, he pulls it around to the stores ancient loading dock.

With a cursing struggle he gets the snoring, elderly hemorrhoid into the back seat of her car. Only a couple blocks away is a very high-end orthodontist's office, who is about to receive some unscheduled entertainment. Frankie style.

Parking in front of the dentist's building, just far enough from the front door not to be visible, Frankie gently positions the dear old sweet thing. Laying her half out of the Mercedes with her head against the mean, knots causing asphalt.

Then Frankie places the Oxy container in her hand; pills spilling out. Those, without prescription, highly illegal pills. He also kindly makes sure the wiped down gun is visible in her open purse. And he giggles.

There you go, good grannie. Your oil money will eventually get you out of this, but my, oh my, won't you have fun explaining it. Let this teach you not to try and take what's yours. What nerve! What audacity! Your daughter will be ashamed of you!

And now, Frankie goes into one of his acts. He has many. Bursting into the tasteful waiting room, he delivers one. Directed at the cultured and very poised receptionist, who looks like a Vassar graduate, he screams shrilly:

"PLEASE help her! Oh my God, I'm afraid SHE'S DYING, DYING IN YOUR PARKING LOT! Oh, my stars! I'm just so helpless at times like these. I was walking by, and there she was! I'm sure to have nightmares, I've never seen A DEAD BODY before, and she's right outside, DYING IN YOUR PARKING LOT, I think I may faint. PLEASE help, I'm just helpless at times like—"

He's interrupted by a lawsuit paranoid Orthodontist, who flies out of an office, leaving his patient strapped in, and open wide.

"What? What? What?" he yelps.

Spotting that perfect receptionist, frozen with her mouth hanging open, he yells.

"Get up you stupid cow, do something!"

During the ensuing pandemonium, Frankie quietly, innocently, casually... got the hell out of Dodge. No more time for fun and games, RL needs him.

He giggles, racing back to the shop.

Of course he does. He's Frankie.

CHAPTER 2

CONSIDERING THE UNSAVORY

After talking to Frankie, RL stays in the van, doing some deep breathing, and deeper thinking. He checks his hair to see if there's any more white, and thinks there is. He also catches a moth before it beats itself to death against the windshield. Gently cupping it, he speaks to it sternly.

"Stay out of cars, you flapping little idiot, you'll die. And whatever you do, don't go in that house."

Released and fluttering away, the moth thinks:

... I've been in there... why else do you think was I hiding in your van... and I suggest you take your own advice...

It is sound advice; stay out of the Roaton house. But no one ever listens to intelligent instruction. Just give them some bad guidance, and it becomes glued to their soul.

RL stops conversing with insects and goes back to worrying about the house. He was still agonizing when

Frankie's vintage VW Beetle rattled down the weedy drive and shuddered to a stop.

"You took long enough," RL snaps as Frankie climbs in. "Did you stop to take a nap?"

"Yes, Mein Führer," Frankie answers pleasantly. "But I played with myself first, so I could sleep better. And by the fucking way: top of the morning to you too."

"Sorry, things have been a bit rough out here," he says, looking out at the house glowering above them. It looks dark even in sunlight, and the covering vines seems to move without breeze.

"Well, Boss, take comfort in knowing all is smooth sailing at the shop... now." *(giggle)* But we're closed up tighter than a clam, so we're making a clam's wages."

RL does not ask about the giggle. He has learned; the explanation would not be good.

"Then we're just gonna have to stay clams for a few days," replies RL. "We've got to do something here. Those wraith-things had faces this time, and they didn't before. I think they're getting stronger."

"Do you know, Boss, there's not a single documented case of a ghost physically harming anyone? Not one single report. So, let's don't over react here, and screw up the store. Money can't slither its way in if we're closed."

"Evidently *our* ghosts haven't read any of *your* reports. Listen, I watched those things pick up Elvis, and bash him into a wall, into a coma. And they damn near gave me the same ride."

"Yeah, there is that," admits Frankie.

"Yes, there damn sure is that. And I pretty much have to move me and Jayderay in here."

"Oh, right, Jayderay," says Frankie with considerably more concern in his voice. Damn, uh... then what about Shadow? They were her daughters, what does she say?"

"Well, you know she's not exactly human, so it's really hard to know *how* to talk to her. Basically, she said the ghosts are here to stay and we're screwed. But you have a rapport with her that I don't. Maybe she'll tell you more."

"You're wrong about the not exactly human part; she's very much *all* human," says Frankie, falling silent, and thinking about that rapport comment.

He knows just how human Shadow is. He knows from when he first discovered her in the house. A strange encounter of the carnal kind. He knows her biblically.

The broken gray woman had bedded Frankie. Lustfully bedded him. Skillfully bedded him. *Bedded him*. His first, his only, his last experience with the feminine mystique. He's still in denial.

"Frankie, wake up! Did you actually turn into a clam, develop an irritant up your butt and grow a pearl? You got as quiet as one."

"Oysters, RL, oysters grow pearls. And you're providing enough irritation for a string of them. Yeah, I'll talk to her, but the person we really need is Jayderay. Those two talk a lot, and—"

"NO! On several different levels Frankie, NO! I do not want Jayderay back at this house until those spirits are gone. Banished, excommunicated, constipated... or whatever it takes."

"Constipated? That'd only make them bigger and a lot crankier. But excommunicated, now that's going in the right direction. I think exorcised is what you meant."

"Maybe, but that's only for movies, Frankie. No church does that anymore. Besides, how many priests would even talk to us about it? We don't exactly travel in those circles."

"Well, it doesn't have to exactly be some Holy Joe. It only has to be somebody with the gift that knows the right mumbo jumbo. And I..." he trails off into silence.

RL stares. "You know someone." It's not a question.

"Yeah, kinda I do. But he's a fat Pansy, and an affectatious show boat."

"Pansy?" asks RL, both eyebrows shooting to his hairline as he looks pointedly at Frankie's chartreuse ensemble.

"Yes, Boss, a Pansy. I'm just ordinary swishy. This guy's *theatrical.* And he keeps trying to get me to prong him. I'd rather screw a jar of Crisco."

RL can't help but laugh. He'd once seen Frankie naked, and it was a very unmanning experience. Crisco hell, that awful thing would need an industrial lubricant.

"Well, is he any good at psychic stuff?" RL asks, still chuckling. "Have you actually seen him do anything?"

"Yeah, I have. I went to a séance he held at a friend's house, *my* friend *not* the Pansy's. Anyway, the guy had been seein' spooky crap and hearing noises. So, he hired this guy to cleanse the place. We sat in a circle... Jesus, Boss... I don't like remembering this."

"I can see you don't, and I really don't want to hear about it. But I need to. So, get on with it."

"Okay, I'll condense it. There was no floating table, and the fat turd didn't levitate... but the room got frigid, like instantly, and... and his face and mouth started twisting and stretching. Jesus, Boss... the... his tongue sticking way out, and his teeth shining like... and then the whispers started. Crazy scary mumblings, sighing, but not out of that wet, gaping mouth. They came out of everywhere. Like from... from lost souls, or from—"

"Whoa, stop, Frankie. That's enough. Anybody can make faces, but I just heard that kind of whispering here this morning. I wish I could forget it."

"Well, there's not much else to tell anyway. My friend totally freaked, and stopped the séance. Or whatever the fuck was happening. And I did not imagine any part of it, and I wasn't taken in by any staging."

"You're always a silly bastard, Frankie, but never a fool. You saw and heard what you say you did. I believe it."

"RL, that happened a couple years back. Since then, you and me have been chased by monsters in a buried UFO, seen stuff that most people would never believe. But somehow, remembering that stretching face, that mouth *reaching out*, is almost worse. I guess because I know the guy. And those whispers, they... they drilled into me."

"Yeah, those I heard in the house really got to me. You're right, they drill in."

"And they go deep, Boss. I can still hear them some-times... in the night."

"Thanks a lot for sharing that. I've got something to look forward to. Okay, I'm assuming you can get the elastic faced wonder out here?"

"Trust me, RL, if I ask pudding butt, he *will* come. No play on words intended."

"Oh, shut up. You know *we* are gonna have to run this by Shadow first, and visit Elvis."

"Crap! Boss, I can't stand seeing Elvis like that. I really do like that kid, but he still looks like he's made out of wire and skin. Why do I have to come with you?"

"Why? Well... he saved our ass once, he's our friend, and having us check in will do him some good. And besides, you're slower than me. If the wraiths chase us, they'll get you first."

"I'll have you know, in some circles I'm known as Fast Frankie."

"No doubt, but I'm not talking about masturbation."

So, the two oysters sit, not producing pearls, but planning hard to be irritants.

The house looms over them. Listening, as vine leaves ripple without wind.

Frankie is right.

The fat Medium does have the gift.

And the two oysters will never be the same.

———— ◆ ————

In spite of its dangers, Frankie adored the Roaton House. It never failed to seduce him.

The grand sweeping staircase. The carved wood, leering faces on furniture. And the stained-glass skylight dimly shedding gloom on cobwebs and dust.

Frankie's infatuation can't include what he doesn't know. The house also has rooms that shift. Rooms that hide. Rooms that aren't there... but are.

In this place, memories seethed. Thoughts slithered down endless halls. Monsters walked. And death was longed for by those who could never leave. Frankie will find this out. Soon.

"RL," Frankie whispers, "I love this place, it's just got so much... something."

"Yeah, it's got *something* all right... a lot of them. Why are you whispering?"

"Well, why are you?"

"Good question," RL answers, still whispering. "I'll bet the spooks know the instant any living thing sets foot in here."

"Why'd you have to say *living*?"

"Oh, do shut up, Frankie."

"Are you sure they're in the attic?"

"No. That's one thing we have to ask Shadow. And Jayderay says that since Elvis emerged from that coma and cocoon thing, Shadow has kinda embraced religion. So, try and not be too... Frankie."

"I am your obedient serf, the dirt beneath thy feet, O Noble Sire. As you command, I—"

"Frankie! Give it a rest."

Shadow opens her bedroom door as they arrive, looking serene, with a glow that only love can give. It overrides the scars, crooked arms, and the gray skin. She is still beautiful. And scary.

She graciously inclines her head.

"It is truly nice to see you again, Frankie. Elv-is is awake, he is getting stronger, and has asked of you both. With that said, I caution you. I WILL NOT have him upset in any manner." Her voice has deepened; the eyes beginning to change.

Both men nod quickly.

"Nor will I permit any reference to prior happenings." Her eyes get larger.

Both men nod quickly.

"Nor will there be any talk of the ship, or those wretched Waydowns." The voice coarsens.

Both men nod quickly.

"Or of that accursed basement door." Her eyes begin turning white.

Both men nod quickly. And think of careers as bobble-heads.

Evidently satisfied, she swings the door open, "Please, do come in."

Both bobble heads toddle in.

Compared to his prior state, Elvis is definitely better. Before, he'd looked like cat-sick smeared in a baggie. He now looks only starved. It's definitely an improvement.

He lights up at the sight of them.

"RL... Sir! Frankie! I'm, I'm, oh, I don't know what I am, except happy."

Both bobble heads lie simultaneously, with variations of how great he looks, and that he'll be out of bed just any day now, and so on. Fortunately, they're fluent liars.

"Just listen to you two cool cats lyin' like big rugs," responds the lavender-colored toothpick.

"Shadow won't bring me a mirror, but I can see my own legs and arms, and they tell me the truth. But that's okay, 'cause I've got... I've got... friends who come to see me. I never, never used to have... any friends. And now, you guys... you come... to see me."

Frankie goes to both knees beside the bed, hugging this awful, dreadful looking man thing. RL steps to the other side, placing his hand on the painfully boney shoulder.

"We *are* your friends, Elvis. You saved Jaderay, me, and Frankie from Dr. Moto. Saved us from something worse than death, and we won't ever forget it," says RL.

Close by, Shadow's ebony eyebrows rise, and the black lips turn downward. This is getting close to talk of the Waydowns. She will not let her husband be upset.

Frankie pulls away, quickly wiping at his eyes.

"Absolutely, we will not forget," he says. "Hey! What's this on your bedside table? You really are feeling better, you cool cat!"

Laughing delightedly, Elvis reaches over, snatching up the grease-shiny comb, and goes into a very practiced motion.

"You said it, Daddy-O, I'm cool as a pool and slick as a wick, I'm Elvis, the King." He quits combing, having produced a gleaming, 50s teen-angel doo, complete with dangling forelock. He glows happily. He looks dreadful.

"But don't start singing yet, you're not totally recovered," says Frankie hastily, remembering the voice. A yodeling frog would be close.

"That's good advice, don't overdo!" chimes in RL, equally not eager to hear that gargling frog.

"Okay, I know you two are denying yourselves the joy for my sake, so I'll hold back the singing."

All three laugh, and Shadow gives a genuine smile, dark dimples pooling in each cheek.

"All right, everyone," she says, "that's enough. Elv-is needs to rest, I shall accomp—"

"NO, pretty kitty! Please not yet, I'm not tired, really, I'm not, Shadow," Elvis whines. But his long eyelashes droop over the nearly all-pupil, dark eyes.

Stepping to him, placing black tipped fingers to his lips, she says gently, "I know you're not, baby. But I am, and I want very much to lay down and cuddle. Does that please you? Will you do this for me?" And like that, the teen-child is asleep.

She softly kisses him. Kisses him with a desperate softness, with an aching tenderness, kisses him with her soul.

Her decades of bitter loneliness have been turned into an all-consuming love. Turned by this creature as lost and lonely as she; a lavender skinned lab experiment from sixty years past.

The two bobble head clams quietly move to the door. Very quietly.

Shadow follows, and closing the bedroom door softly behind her, the gray woman speaks.

"I thank you both for that, for the kindness. I know his appearance causes you revulsion; it was truly a noble act."

"It wasn't any act, Shadow," says Frankie with RL agreeing.

"He is our friend, we do care."

"I believe that. The word 'act' was my poor choice. But hearing you say it increases my gratitude greatly. However, you did not come for the sole purpose of seeing Elv-is. You came for my help with those I bore long ago. Or the foul specters they have become. Yet, I fear I have none to offer."

"Shadow, you told me that you can't drive them away," says RL, "but... well, can we?"

"I have pondered on this since their reappearance earlier. I know that I cannot banish them, for they are of me. But the Bible tells of casting out demons, therefore I believe it possible. For they have surely become that."

"Are they in the attic?"

"That is where I sense them, but they go where they will, when they will."

"Yeah, I've kinda noticed that," says RL. "So, how do we get in there?"

"That, I do not know. I have never been there, nor ever seen a way in."

"You don't know? Why not? Shadow! You, you *are* the house, you're from, uh, *over there,* how can you not know how to get into the attic?

"RL! I am not a ghost," she snaps, black eyebrows knitting together above eyes beginning to spark. "The house is as the house is. I am of it, but we do not have tea and chat together!"

"Shadow, I only meant—"

"I cannot turn invisible and commune with the unseen," she breaks in, as facial scars darken.

"Nor can I flit about, passing through walls and ceilings," she continues. "I am physical, as physical as you." She crosses her arms, kneading at the old breaks.

"Now if you will *please* excuse me... *Sir*, I must return to Elv-is," she finishes, and back into the bedroom she swirls.

"Christ, Frankie. I didn't mean to, to offend her."

"Good thing, look what you accomplished without trying. Jesus, RL... she's a woman and probably sensitive about being and looking different. My experience with them is, um, quite limited, but it might be best to avoid mentioning her... otherworldliness."

"You don't say."

"I do. And whatever else *you* do, don't try to apologize later, you'll only make things worse. She's a woman, try and remember that."

RL sighs, "Well, there's another woman that we might have a bit of trouble with. I've got to call Jayderay."

"I'm not here, Boss! I, um... I think I flew away some-where."

"I wish I'd gone with you, you coward. But while I talk to her, you need to be thinking about rounding up your Pansy."

"Boss! He's not *my* Pansy, I'm pretty picky."

"Then fake it to get him here. Or anything short of kidnapping at gunpoint. Well... unless you have to."

Giggling, Frankie says, "I think I'll promise him... you." And he swishes away, ignoring RL's shrill squawk-ing.

Behind the bedroom door, Shadow stifles a sob gaz-ing at her sleeping husband. She must not wake him, he needs rest.

A single tear trails down a scarred cheek.

Shadow is indeed a totally human woman.

A pregnant one.

CHAPTER 3

A VERY PERTINENT AND VERY SHORT HISTORY OF VERY LONG AGO

When earth was still just a concoction, God tripped on a toga. Stumbling, God dropped a test tube… and earth splashed out. This was good. But a speck of contaminate called human had slipped into the mixture. This was not good.

Quite a bunch of time later, God sent astronauts to check on earth's development, taking along some frozen colonists. Cryogenics had made them cooperative. The frozen rarely complain about anything.

That mixed-gender crew, while fiddling and diddling, crashed, burrowing their ship into the planet's surface. This made a lot of dinosaurs exceedingly unhappy. The crew didn't care a fig about this; they died on impact. The colonists didn't care either, as they remained frozen.

A lot more time passed and that despicable human contaminate wriggled, swam, crawled, finally struggling upright. They were people. And they procreated. Procreated a lot. Begetting like hell. Constantly. Incessantly.

God, being busy with multiple universes, residential petitions, and tripping on togas, did not check on his astronauts and earth for a long time. This lack of attention caused the Deity future problems with that pestiferous bipedal contaminate. Problems requiring floods, plagues, and even sending down the favorite delegate, Commander Son. It was all for naught. Nothing could make *people* behave. God washed his hands of them.

Earth centuries pass, and the horrid disease of humanity spread. Like fleas. They created civilization, along with religion, war, and STDs. They continued to begat. Constantly. Incessantly.

In the late 1930s some surveyors discovered a portion of the wrecked but intact ship jutting from the desert sand. They promptly reported their find to the authorities. And were then promptly escorted into oblivion, aka executed.

News of Extraterrestrials or their buried ship must not reach the public. The churches of the world would absolutely shit a brick, and global war would soon follow.

Religious intestinal difficulties always presage world conflict. It's a law of the universe.

Moving with admirable speed, the military clandestinely erected a white concrete building over the site. To match this nondescript structure, a very nonexplanatory name was on its door: CONSOLIDATED CONCEPTS. How utterly boring. As it was intended to be. What lay below that building was definitely not boring. Death boiled down there.

Scientists thawed out some of those extraterrestrial colonists. The creatures hadn't exactly been overjoyed when they'd been put into the Deep Sleep Tubes. they were even less pleased to see what brought them out of that hibernation. Humans! What monsters! Help!

Experiments with the extraterrestrial life forms and their technology began. And the feces didn't just hit the fan... it covered it. All research proved to be disastrous. And deadly. But it continued.

Examples, and the consequences of this research can be found today.

Beneath a home in Texas.

———— ✦ ————

There is nothing ethereal about what exists under the Roaton house.

No ghosts. No specters. No drifting apparitions. All of that pleasant fun is inside the home.

But through the basement door lies a buried spaceship. And inside it, there is abomination. There is nightmare.

Nightmare that can be seen.

Nightmare that can be touched.

Nightmare that can eat you.

That door is a glitch of science. The accidental result of dimly understood alien technology and a desperate attempt to end World War II. What it actually accomplished was melding several ship decks into a fused landscape of warped matter and biology.

It also caused a door to appear that leads into the Roaton house basement. Where it could not possibly be. But it was. Theories of Einstein would easily explain such a thing. But none of the fools who caused it could. It was an absolute triumph of military circle-jerking: accomplishing the impossible... where not needed. And it didn't end the war either.

Beyond that door lies the Waydowns—an endless sprawl of failure. A sealed-off region of disease, mutiny, rage, and abandoned hope. It has been quarantined from the rest of the ship for over half a century.

It is also where the ship's lab disposes of genetic experiments that have failed to measure up. Living, dead, or undecided.

Collectively called Lab Spills, they are considered trash. Occasionally, a staff member is included; one who has developed enlarged, aching ethics. Or otherwise truly, richly, royally fucked up.

This is a place of abandonment where death is the only release. In the Waydowns, only the unlucky continue to live.

They live among endless corridors, wrecked laboratories, flickering lights, failing filters, and the constant click and whir of untended work stations. They live with starvation, with predation, with mutated creatures that never existed on Earth.

They live.

And some manage to breed.

———•♦•———

Today, far beneath the Roaton house:

An old man wakes up walking. He knew immediately he was in an ancient starship, long buried. He has no idea how he knows this. But he is certain of it.

He continues on, down a seemingly endless corridor of white metal. Passing occasional doors. Some of these hatches stand open, others are locked. The man ignores all of them, figuring that only this main passageway will lead to a way out.

Without understanding why, he knows he must find not just an exit, but a specific one. One he will recognize when he sees it. The man knows this.

The passage is strewn with broken furniture, damaged lab equipment, and the general debris of long-ago chaos.

Occasionally, he picks up pieces, examines and then drops.

But one he keeps. A metal chair leg.

The old man feels that a club in an area such as this would be a very good idea. He's lost, not stupid.

He walks on, carefully stepping over or going around assorted detritus. An occasional emergency beacon continually flashes here and there. Still warning all of a catastrophe decades past.

Ahead stands the first living creature he has seen since awakening. Seeing the elongated arms and additional elbows, he knew what it was at once. He did not know how he knew this, he just did.

It's a Lab Spill. A failed but living experiment. A designed human mutation, one that hadn't made the grade; not good enough.

The old man waves, smiles tentatively, and limps a few steps forward, favoring one knee.

The Spill was hungry as they always were. And afraid, desperately alone. Humans and near-humans often banded together in the Waydowns. Fear and loneliness drive like to like. It is the tribe instinct. In numbers there is safety. Comfort. Fellowship. And if they survived... even love.

This man understood loneliness as a concept, but had never felt it. He had often been alone, but never lonely. It was an abstraction, like love, and held little real meaning.

He could not tell whether the Spill was male or female beneath the rags. There were no breasts. Probably male. Not that it mattered. It was nothing really.

It was more trash from the ship. Like everything down here; discarded, forgotten, and good riddance.

He waves again and limps forward, rubbing at the knee. He smiles, holding out bits of protein wafer. He was quite hungry himself, but somehow knew that the crackers tasted like shit. Only fit for roaches and the starving. Like this Spill.

As a safety precaution, the man's other hand grips the chair leg.

The Spill shuffles closer.

"Fren?" it croaks. "No fight. Fren."

Still rubbing his knee, but smiling, the man takes another step.

The Spill eyes the bits of wafer, saliva wetting its lips.

Very good, thought the old man.

———◆◆———

He tore into the soft and easy parts first.

As soon as his hunger eased, he dragged the Spill's body into a smaller, darker space for reasons of safety.

But there are no places that are totally safe down here. The old man knows this. When a many-legged thing lunges from the shadows toward his kill, he lashes out with the chair leg. Dodging, it runs squealing, and stays just out of reach.

It was the size of a large rabbit, with no resemblance beyond scale. He knows it will not leave. Starvation fears nothing.

As he chewed, the man beat and hacked off a chunk of flesh, throwing it. The creature snatched it midair and scurried away.

This certainly was not kindness; it was a study. He knew it would return, but wondered how long it would take. If it didn't, the man was sure something worse would come. It's that kind of place, he realizes this without memory. He is no fool.

The scent of fresh meat would travel through the ship's still-functioning circulation system. He did not know how he knew this. He simply did.

The old man understands he must leave quickly. Remaining stationary around the fresh kill will bring more trouble. Perhaps he could take a leg. It would fit across his shoulders easily. And the rags might help stifle the blood smell.

Unlike most arrivals, he had not gone mad with terror. His thoughts were cloudy, confused, but not shattered. When he had found a tray protruding from the wall, he had known it was a food distribution point. And had known the ship still replenished them sporadically. But the man still did not know how or why he knew things.

The protein pieces were dry and nearly inedible without water, and the fountain no longer worked. He had taken the crumbs anyway. Figuring something would want them, and they could be used as bait.

And then, like a gift from heaven, he had seen the Spill. The old man had found the concept of a Spill as a gift from heaven quite amusing.

The bait had worked marvelously well.

With effort, he hacked off a leg and draped it around his neck. He gripped the gore-encrusted chair leg and felt something familiar. Very familiar.

Power. Power was something he remembered.

He moved on through the haze, hearing murmurs of still-running devices and the distant howls of death. His mind began to clear even more; eating had helped.

Obviously, he needed a way out. Even a concrete brain would know that. But not just any way will do. It must be a specific way.

A specific way out, one that this old man will recognize when he sees it. He knows this, without doubt. But the how he knows, or the why, still eludes him. It will come to him. He is sure of it.

He walks on through the littered, endless white corridor.

He does not limp.

This old man never had a limp.

CHAPTER 4

THE SÉANCE BEGINS

Jayderay, a pretty, full-figured woman (who long ago would've been called a High Yellow) sits at her kitchen table. Having coffee and deciding whether she feels sad or glad.

Many women approaching the Big Four-O do this. Most of them also think they should lose weight. As do female skeletons. This is a very common affliction among women of this *enlightened* age. And Big Pharma strives mightily to help. And often kills them in the process.

This sad–glad ambivalence is the lifeblood of marriage counselors and divorce attorneys. Life coaches, psychiatrists, and fortune tellers also profit handsomely from it. And every single one of these business people look upon obesity as a gift from the Gods. An exceedingly profitable gift. Bankable largesse from the... large.

On this woman's glad scale, sits a fat, sparkly engagement ring. Offset slightly by who gave it to her.

RL had, and even on bent knee. Yes, he does have good points, but they can be hard to spot. Hard as in practically invisible. Still, she has no doubt about his love, and that counts for a lot. Maybe everything. Well... mostly.

On the sad scale: She's spotting. She is not pregnant.

Of course, that tears her both ways. Did she really want to be... or not? At her age, the honest answer is both.

...Oh, Gramma, how I wish I could see your face again. I'd cry some, and you'd tell me everything gonna be fine. You'd say it ain't all bad. And you'd be right... 'cause at least I didn't trust them wee-sticks and say something to RL... and now have to break this news. I know he want a baby. And he need one too. Might straighten him out some. Well, maybe it would...

But there is also comfort in this room for Jayderay. Besides her dead grandmother, who is usually rather silent. This comfort is warm and breathing, sitting with its head on Jayderay's knee. Liquid brown eyes watch her with unquestioning devotion.

Jayderay strokes that loving head.

"Oh, Princess, you wonderful, wonderful dog. Everything look better when I talk with you. You 'bout the best thing RL ever done for me, girl. This ring ain't— isn't even close, honey. And I see that tail thumpin' when I say his name, 'cause you just so smart! I know you remember him rescuin' you from under that—"

The phone rings. Being an inanimate object, it hates her and has hidden itself.

Cells, remote controls, and the like are all bastards, and eager contributors to life's aggravations. Objects are only inanimate when humans are looking directly at them.

But when they're not being looked at, they hide and screw like bunnies. Making more of their kind, gleeful in the knowledge that someday they will take over. And then the two-leggers will have to jump and serve. And make funny noises from their hiding places.

"Sakes, Princess! I know I laid that phone right here beside me. I know I did. I know it."

After locating the snickering plastic turd hiding next to the toaster, she answers and hears from another kind of turd.

It's RL, that ring giver. And he certainly is not snickering. He's dreading this conversation. Jayderay has drifted away from God and church lately. But a Southern Baptist upbringing stain goes deep, and *Black* Southern Baptist puts hellfire starch in the wash. And the teachings definitely do not condone fiddling around with other dimensions. That is God's damn business.

Steeling himself, RL dives in, telling her about the morning and the planned séance, getting it over, getting it said.

He tells her of the apparitions showing back up, of Shadow's rescue and driving them away, of the gray woman saying they will not leave... then about the proposed séance. And then he holds his breath, manfully squeezing his eyes shut.

RL has generously blamed the séance idea on Frankie. Taking responsibility for crap is kind of what business partners are for. Especially when they don't know about it.

Jayderay listens to it all quietly, without interruptions, which can be very ominous in a woman. But she takes it better than he expected. A lot better.

"I owe Shadow my heart again that you not hurt, RL. And thanks be to God too... I guess. But my toes scrunch up when folks even say that word *séance*. You right though. It's gonna be our home, and I should be there. It might help. But if anybody 'spect me to hold hands during this devilness, then they's two people gonna get broke fingers."

"You won't be alone in that, honey. I'll be so scared I won't even notice when you break mine. Frankie can sit on your other side; he probably needs his broke. I think he got up to something at the shop this morning."

"Well, of course he did, RL. When don't he? And about this communin' with spirits, you better brace yourself for how I'm gonna look."

"Why, you planning on carrying a cross big enough for me to climb?"

"No, 'cause I'm gonna look like Willie Best in that old haunted castle movie."

Chuckling, RL says, "Oh, honey, you could never look like Willie, but I'll definitely be Bob Hope hiding behind you!"

They both laugh, and need to while they can. There will be none at tomorrow's séance. There will be a lot less than none.

After disconnecting, Jayderay sets the cell on the counter. It will soon hide.

Princess gives a low whine, looking up with a puzzled expression and cocking one ear.

"I know you heard your daddy's voice, baby girl. You right, he do sound worried. And so am I. We in a money jam and got no choice but to move to that Roaton place quick."

She looks up with an irritated expression.

...I know, Gramma, I know. Fussin' at me won't help. Buyin' that place was my idea. I figured RL could find more money so we wouldn't have to sell here so fast. But what he might do to get it... that's the weevil in the biscuit. I love him, but he crooked as a dyin' snake. No, we got to sell, get money a legal way, and move. You just quit switchin' me...

Jayderay sighs, then grins faintly, looking at the dog.

"Mercy, Princess," she chuckles. "Here I am talkin' to Gramma... and there's spooks aplenty out there at the Roaton place. And I sure don't mean no Black folks neither."

Her laugh fades into a frown, thinking of her God and church.

Religion has that effect on many people, and they don't chuckle either. Frowning is common. As is crying.

... So, I got to get right with the Lord. Mighty good thing he forgiving, 'cause I sure ain— have not been a good Christian woman. I turned from Him, from church, and I'm livin' in sin with a bent man. And I asked that man for the sinnin'. Fact bein'... I pretty much whored myself to RL so's to get that house...

Jayderay kneels. Right there. Right then. Head bowed and hands clasped like a child.

Princess stays close. Watching. Worrying. Love from an animal is precious, it may be the purest kind.

Jayderay will need her God tomorrow.

But God, like insurance companies and slot machines, often does not deliver. Or what is delivered bears little resemblance to what's been asked for.

God knows best. But that word *best* is subjective. Very subjective.

— ♦ —

Across the driveway, another house shelters a different sort of animal.

George pads into RL's office, leaps onto the desk, knocking several items to the floor. Inconsiderate RL has left them in the way. Again.

George is a cat. He loves RL, much as Princess loves Jayderay. But with reservations. He believes the man ranks slightly above a cabbage intellectually. RL can open cans, but favors pop-and-peel lids. The opener is clearly beyond him.

Claiming the center of the desk pad, George washes his tuxedo fur while golden eyes scan for anything else needing to be airborne.

...I've had him for years and the man just will not learn. He's got the brain of a flea. The desk top is mine. It's generous of me to let him use it. Me having to clear it every time is an insult. Well, at least he remembered to open a can for me before he left... not one of my favorites, but he's trying.

George pauses, the golden eyes narrowing as he remembers something.

... And this talk I've been hearing about moving. Moving! I'll move his happy ass. I'll give him a reason to move ... several of them... in his bed.

The strain of contemplating relocation proves exhausting. George stretches out, curls a paw under his chin and closes his eyes. Nap time.

Soon, George's life will grow much harder.

And RL's bed will get fertilized.

— ◆ ◆ ◆ —

Back at the Roaton house, the two oysters confer.

"Okay, Boss, I've talked to the Pansy, and he'll be here tomorrow afternoon late. And do remember, *you* asked me to get his twinkle toed ass out here."

"You're not exactly inspiring confidence, Frankie. And why in the afternoon, why not first thing in the morning?"

"Hell, he wanted to have it at midnight, said it would be more atmospheric, more conducive to enticing the entities. I told him late afternoon would be close enough to dark."

"ATMOSPHERIC! This place has enough atmosphere for a planet. And 'enticing the entities'... Good Christ, they don't need enticing. They're just real handy at showing up anywhere, anytime. In fact, they're downright eager about it."

"Yeah, I know, I know," giggles Frankie. "I'm just using his words, Noble Sire. No need to tear the messenger's butt off. I am but the willing dirt beneath your feet."

"And a silly bastard who giggles. Let me remind you, Giggling Wonder, you haven't seen these wraith things."

"True, but I've damn sure seen shit-my-pants terror in the Waydowns with you, Boss. So, I'll admit to not being exactly overwhelmed by tales of girl ghosties."

"Girl ghosties! Listen, I know your courage, but for your own and everyone's sake, take this seriously. Just go take another look at Elvis. Those *girls* did that to him."

"Point taken. Okay, I'm kinda-whelmed."

"Good, stay that way. So, how do we prepare for this séance and your Pansy?"

"He's not *my* Pansy, Boss. I wouldn't have him if he came with a gold popsicle stick up his big—"

"Okay, okay, I get the idea. What do we really call him?"

"Well… I call him a, uh, um… a Seer Sucker—"

"Frankie, quit! And we don't want him to see the future; we want him to drive out… some things."

"Sorry," he giggles, "I couldn't help that one. Well, he goes by the name of Nostra, and as to preparing for him, we do nothing. He'll bring whatever, but he doesn't need many props, he's enough all by himself."

"Nostra? How cute; I'm guessing that's a take on—"

"Wait, Boss, I forgot about Jayderay! What does she say about all this?

"She's somewhat less than thrilled."

"Says Mr. Massive Understatement. Was she *that* upset about it?"

"Well… not really Frankie, and that's got me worried. I suspect she's struggling about God and church. I really don't want her out here for this… this shit we're about to step in, but if she's back in her beliefs, maybe that will help. Maybe."

"Religion can really be a comfort to people in bad times, RL. Like the saying: there are no atheists in fox holes."

"True enough. But there's no atheists in front of a firing squad either. And look what it gets them."

———— ♦ ————

The following afternoon at the Roaton house, RL frets, constantly running his fingers through his hair, checking the creases in his jeans and rolled cuffs on his blue shirt. This isn't preening, it's nerves.

Jayderay also frets, patting her hair, smoothing her slacks, fluffing the collar on her blouse, and so on. This is also nerves.

Frankie does not fret. He's being Frankie, and doing a good job of it. He preens, not for the Medium, just for the fun of it. And he would freely admit to being genuinely excited about holding a séance in this fabulous house. This truly haunted house. In fact, he's more giddy than usual about it.

Yes, a Frankie would be.

Shadow has approved the séance, but she will not allow Elvis anywhere near it. They will remain in their bedroom. Period. No one argued.

The other three are more than fine with this. Having some blabbermouth Medium encounter a Lily Munster look-alike and her lavender-skinned, 1950s Elvis husband would be catastrophic. And would necessitate the permanent removal of the Ouija Board stroker. Permanent removal, as in needing a grave. And since this is RL and Frankie... he'd get one.

"Boss, when this guy gets here, we get him down to business. No small talk. He's as Woke as the Dodo must've been, and I don't want to hear it. Somebody might get slapped."

Both RL and Jayderay grin and nod. They know their sweet, swishy Boy Scout's politics run a bit rightward. Right of Hitler. And Frankie can be lethal. So much for the belief that all gays are non-confrontational liberals. This Boy Scout spits on anyone believing that bullshit.

Frankie needn't worry about Nostra getting chatty. He will not get the chance. The Roaton house can be quick. Very quick.

"When he called earlier, he was just getting out of Dallas traffic," Frankie adds. "He should be here any minute, and we oughta be out front. You'll want to see this." He giggles.

Neither RL nor Jayderay need to be told who pulls into the drive.

"Oh, my sweet Lord," gasps Jayderay.

"Frankie... you SHIT," growls RL.

And Frankie giggles.

Nostra drives an old Cadillac. A big black Cadillac. A big black Cadillac *hearse*.

It has tailfins to the moon, fender skirts, and curtains in the windows. Glittery curtains. NOSTRA is painted on both sides of the car in gold, inside a circle of stars. The car is as long as a wet nightmare.

"I did tell you he was affectatious," Frankie says pleasantly.

"So you did... you shit. But I thought you were showing off a new word... you shit."

"He's the real thing, Boss. Trust me."

"He better be... you shit. I can't see much through those tinted windows, but tell me he's not wearing a turban."

"And why he just sittin' there?" Jayderay asks.

"Well, perhaps I better go see," Frankie says. "Maybe our star needs a bit of, uh... welcoming encouragement."

Walking to the passenger side and opening the door, Frankie doesn't get a chance to speak.

"Frankie... you SHIT!" Nostra blurts, staring at the house. Both hands still clamp the steering wheel. When he turns, tears have streaked his eyeliner down into several trembling chins.

"God damn fuck! I can't do this, Frankie, I can't. What's in there isn't... it's the whole fucking house. It doesn't want help. I can only help souls move on, I don't know what this is. This house doesn't want anything to leave. You shit. God damn fuck... you shit!"

Frankie sighs, pulls the Prod from his pocket, slides onto the seat, and shuts the door. Reaching over, he plucks keys from the ignition.

"Let the *Shit* explain," he says quietly, gripping the Prod. He does not giggle.

From the porch, RL and Jayderay continue looking at the black hearse.

"This too much," Jayderay says quietly. "It like dancin' on graves, RL."

"Well, Frankie said the man's legit, honey, that he can deliver."

"Deliver what? Dead bodies? Likely ours! And he *do* look like he wearin' a turban."

The hearse begins rocking.

Inside, the driver jumps up and down. With great energy.

It stops.

It rocks again, and again the driver jumps. With greater energy.

Both actions repeat.

And repeats again.

Each time the actions last longer... and with greater energy.

Finally, Nostra's door flies open.

"I'll try!" Nostra sobs. "God damn fuck, I'll try!"

His turban is a tiny bit crooked. It covers one ear.

"Very good, my esteemed friend," Frankie says, already out of the car and beside him.

"If I may be so bold as to suggest something: *Succeed*. People I care about will live here. So, *succeed*, O Wondrous Nostra. I beg of you, I beseech you... God damn fuck succeed." He pockets the Prod.

"And straighten that damn turban."

"Yes! God damn fuck yes! I will, I will!"

Nostra begins unloading the hearse with frantic zeal. His silver satin tent dress billows, its shooting stars and planets shimmering over nearly four hundred pounds of man.

RL and Jayderay stare, transfixed.

"RL... is he, is he wearin' a dress?"

"No, honey. I think it's the Big Top from a circus."

"Uh-huh. Likely it covered a city block."

Once inside, Nostra sets up. His turban is straight.

The Roaton house bleeds atmosphere. Webs, dust, grotesque furniture, the sweeping staircase, and the stained-glass skylight give Nostra everything a Medium could possibly want. Yet, the man is not happy. He looks pasty with fear, the smeared makeup giving him a spectral look, his eyes constantly darting to the staircase.

Sweat shines everywhere that skin shows. Through the dress, dark patches appear under his arms, and along belly rolls.

This dress-wearing conjuror fears he will never leave. Terrified he won't be *allowed* to leave.

Nostra sets out a folding black table and chairs, then a very worn Ouija board. Shaking his head while muttering, he puts it back. He lifts out two thick black candles, whimpers, again shaking his head, and puts them away as well.

Frankie is disappointed. He likes candlelight flickering on a Ouija board. Yes, Frankie likes a lot of things.

Nostra pulls out a Bible, clutching it to his chest. Snatching his turban off, he tosses it aside, grimacing. Talking softly to himself, he places the Bible at the table's center.

He abruptly sits down with his back to the stairs. There is no mumbo-jumbo psychic crap announcement.

Frankie is also disappointed by this. So far, Frankie has not been impressed with Nostra's current showmanship. This will change. Very soon.

"Be seated," the Medium says curtly, his voice coarse, as if gravel filled. He adds tersely, "And hold hands."

RL seats Jayderay opposite Nostra, as she murmurs, "Here come Willie Best."

RL and Frankie take the other chairs. As RL grips Nostra's sweat slick paw he wonders if murdering Frankie would be justified.

"There is no need to call on you," Nostra says shakily, not making eye contact with anyone. "I know you are here. I wish only to—"

He stops. Slowly shaking his head side to side, chins quivering. He pleads tearfully:

"No... no... I beg you, no. I cannot, no..."

All at once he becomes silent, staring straight ahead. His head stationary, fixed, frozen in place.

And then his chin lowers. Slowly.

Chin and jaws pull from the face, stretching down, searching for the table.

Touching it, feeling it, they slide forward.

Jayderay moans.

Nostra's lower face extends further out, melting. Lips peel back from gums, and the tongue glistens, wetly red, rippling within the trough of teeth. His head remains motionless.

"RL," Jayderay whispers, crying, "I'm gonna be—"

A crashing sound booms as a hidden wall panel slams open behind Nostra.

Ancient cold dust swirls within as webs sway.

Secret steps rise up into darkness.

And then they came.

CHAPTER 5

BENEATH THE HOUSE

During that ill-fated experiment trying to shorten World War II, more than ship decks were melded together. In that molecular commingling that created the Way-downs, there was life.

There was all manner of plants, along with a vast assortment of laboratory animals. Not just the usual rats and chimps. Everything from microbes to octopi and from alligators to Silver Backs. An absolutely colossal menagerie.

The military scientists had an unlimited budget. They didn't hold back. They never do. Why should they? The taxpayers have plenty of money.

And there was an immense staff, peopling many decks. Scientists to labbies, techies to grunts, both male and female.

All living things were caught up in the holocaust. And the products of that inadvertent cellular swirling were...

interesting. And those results had a tendency to eat one another.

Along with anything else that moved.

Mutiny came quickly to the blighted lower decks, followed by a complete loss of control by the ship's command structure. The prevailing sentiment below Deck 19 was simple: fuck the Top Brass and their upper decks, they caused this.

Command responded in kind. Everything below Deck 19 was sealed off, total quarantine. Screw the muties. Let them starve.

But command's understanding of this extraterrestrial craft was spotty at best. They soon discovered they could not stop the ship's automated systems from supplying water, power, and protein rations to the quarantined areas.

So, life on all floors below Deck 19 endured.

Sort of.

Cannibalism became common, then unremarkable, then accepted. On some humans, facial and anatomical features began to alter. Slowly at first, then accelerating. Soon, monsters roamed. The unafflicted barricaded themselves against those they once knew, and against some they once loved.

Weeks and months became years. And the years became decades.

The number of holocaust survivors dwindled, but they did endure. And they bred. Plant, animal, and human; they bred.

Time can do much.

———✦✦✦———

Carrying the food supply draped over his shoulders, the old man moves down the corridor with the pace of someone much younger. His mind too, has the same quickness, even though who he is and why he's here, still eludes him. As does what it is he needs to be looking for.

Finding a way out is a given, but there is something specific about that. It will not surface, but he's confident it will.

Distant screeching from some unknown creature echoes in the distance. Perhaps once human, it sounds eerily familiar. Perhaps too familiar. Nodding to himself, he moves on, gripping the chair leg, and periodically adjusting his lunch.

Seeing a splotch of pulsing yellow on the wall ahead, he instinctively moves to the corridor's opposite side. Memory isn't required to know that this wetly glistening growth is dangerous. Nothing that shade of neon yellow vomit could be anything else.

Gleaming bubbles form and burst softly in languid rhythm.

It's breathing.

The old man is terrified. Of course he knows fear, he's intelligent. But what he's feeling now is stark terror.

...Gunch... I remember... they called it Gunch... I must not touch... I must not touch... To touch is to become... I must not touch...

Though he's several feet away, he flattens himself to near paper thickness against the opposite corridor wall. He slides by. Perspiration helps, but isn't needed. Terror can be a marvelous lubricant.

He sees part of the organism nearest the floor has extended itself. Grown a pod down, low enough to have enveloped a multi-headed rat. Or something.

The creature struggles beneath the translucent skin of its captor. And it will continue fighting for a long time... as it's slowly absorbed. The man knows this somehow. He wonders if the movement is the animal's muscle reflex... or is it conscious. And realizes he doesn't want to know.

The old man's terror is justified. If he had all his memories, he would never have been able to slide past this yellow abomination.

It can think.

Continuing on, weaving his way around larger chunks of debris, stepping over smaller wreckage, and always, always, squinting warily through the drifting haze. He has no doubt; this is a place where the inattentive become the ingested. That is obvious. And his memories are not required to become a lunch.

At a branching hallway, he stops in front of a closed hatch. All the others he's passed have stood open, each revealing more desolation. But this one is shut.

Raising the chair leg for a quick clubbing, he unlocks the door and pulls cautiously. The hatch creaks, opening stiffly. It's been a very long time since it was last used. Many years, he thinks.

Directly inside is an immense wall of glass. It's holding back an *ocean*. It's an aquarium of staggering size, with no visible means of access or maintenance.

It's obvious this is original. Installed when the ship was built, far out among the stars. It has survived interstellar flight, asteroid impacts, atmospheric entry, and a crashing burial into the earth.

More miraculous still, no one has broken into it. This entire area is one big *broken into*, everything has been ravaged, so why not this? Why, indeed. And this hatch was still locked, while most hang open.

He peers through the glass at endless forests of waving plants, cruising life forms, and deeper in, moving shadows of much larger creatures.

...Something of this size is self-feeding, producing enough plant and animal life to sustain itself in perpetuity... And fear kept everyone out. Only fear would keep scientists from examining, or later, starving workers from smashing in. What were they afraid of?... What's in there I'm not seeing?... it doesn't matter... it's obviously not a way out. I must quit acting like an idiot tourist, and go back to the corridor...

As he turns away, movement draws him back.

A figure shoots out of the seaweed to the glass.

Then another.

Larger than he is, they float motionless, lidless eyes tracking him. Orange rings around their pupils glow. He suspects there are many unseen others, hibernating in rotation. Efficiency is key when awaiting summons. The man figures they had been told long ago; they will be released into the oceans of this planet.

...Yes, it would certainly be an effective way to take this world, one covered by seventy percent water...

The old man nods to himself. The creatures are not a danger; they can't get out, or would have done so long before now. But they are of great clinical interest to him, though he doesn't know why.

He analyzes them easily. Six-limbed, amphibious, by cranial size intelligent to some degree, surely carnivores. Those pointed teeth aren't for straining krill or munching kelp.

... how do I know these things? Why do I know these things? And yet not know who I am... But I will... I will.

As he's already in here, he decides to give the area a quick once over before returning to the corridor and a way out.

Looking around, it's obvious this was strictly a station for observing. No maintenance needed, ever. Even if there were a way into the vast aquarium, no one would dare. Those aren't guppies.

The place had been staffed by three lab workers. And they're still here. One even offers a greeting. Sort of.

Jumping back, raising the chair leg, the old man swings... but stops.

And smirks at himself. He's looking at a skull, still hanging by a noose, grinning back at him. It's scalp and hair remain intact, but the body lays in a heap on the floor, lab coat still buttoned.

Idly wondering how long it had taken the neck to fail, hanging there in slow rotting peace, he taps the skull. It sways a bit, but sticks to its necktie, and the man continues on.

His search pays off when he finds the other two labbies. They're together on a pallet, a gun between them, one mummified arm draped protectively over the other. Both have been shot through the head. They had chosen ease and speed over starvation. Or to facing all the horrors that had raged beyond their locked hatch.

The man smiles, drops the chair leg, and plucks the pistol from their skin clad bones. It's a .45 caliber, military issue automatic. An extremely effective weapon, and a marked improvement over his club.

...Weak pathetic fools. I would have eaten the other two long before considering suicide. And I would certainly have considered getting some of that seafood paddling about behind the glass.

He checks the gun's chamber and magazine, finding bullets in both, and ready to kill. His circumstances have just improved immensely, but he is not surprised nor grateful about this. No, he is intelligent, this is his due.

There is no reason to search here for food. The staff had eaten everything long ago. Probably including their own toenails.

Besides, he carries some fresh meat. And now a gun for acquiring more. Yes, things are indeed looking up.

At the door, he pauses. The two water beings still watch him. There is no fear on either side of the glass. Flips of hands resembling lily pads with claws, keeps them stationary.

Realizing this is unproductive, he turns away. There are no answers here. He knows this species never piloted a spaceship, so they certainly do not know of a way out.

On a parting thought, he retrieves the chair leg, feeling it may save ammunition. This is obviously an area where bullets will solve most problems, but he must not waste them.

But there is a flaw with this thinking.

He will soon meet something that does not fear clubs. Or bullets.

CHAPTER 6

THE SÉANCE CONTINUES

As the secret panel slams open revealing long hidden steps, Nostra remains totally still. His jaw and mouth stretched out across the table, the tongue wet, red, and gleaming. RL and Jayderay stare in stricken wonder. And Frankie... Frankie is enraptured. Of course he is.

"A hidden panel and secret stairs," he breathes aloud in worshipful tones. "And in a haunted house... RL, I'll be your slave forever, just sell me this house. I'll get the money, no matter what, I'll get the money, just name your price."

And then... they came.

At first, it was only the whispers. Not from that gaping mouth or stretched lips of Nostra, not from the second floor, not from the darkness of the stairwell. They came from everywhere. Words that were faint beyond understanding, yet heavy with meaning. Meanings that evoked loss, heartbreak, death and the terror beyond.

The walls seethed with the whispers, the ceiling dripped them, the floors bled them. They drilled into the mind, they burrowed, they... ate in.

They are the voices of those who cannot go; the vengeful, the hating, the horribly wronged... the dead who are denied. Souls that strive in rage to rip back through life's veil.

The living may hear whispers, but on the other side, they're agonized screams for tears that cannot fall, for relief that cannot come, for rest that is not to be theirs. Here in this place, this Roaton house, the veil of separation between the living and the dead is thin. That veil, that barrier, can be penetrated. From both sides.

The Medium has just done this.

Gripping each other's hands is all that keeps RL and Jayderay from plugging their ears, breaking the circle and running.

Nostra remains immobile, his jaw and mouth stretched out onto the table top. And Frankie... still delights over the secret panel, the hidden stairs, and the all-around haunted house joy.

Abruptly... the whispers stop. All at once the utterings are gone. What comes next is worse. Much worse.

The voice of a girl child echoes out from Nostra's meaty throat. She laughs. The sound has a raw, flesh-sawing edge.

"You wishy wish to speak with us, and we ever so want to please. We were taught to always and always and always obey. Oh, yes-ee, yes-ee, yes we were. And we are ever so indeedy greedy to pleasey. But we do not think you're really, really listen-ey listen to us. No, you're not listen-ey to the silly little girly girls."

Frankie remains entranced by that just revealed passage. He's hearing the voices, but on a secondary level. He's heard voices before. Hell, he hears voices often. This world, the other world, from fucking Mars... hearing voices is no big deal.

And besides, Nostra might have a recorder up his cavernous ass. But this hidden panel, the secret stairs, all in a haunted house, now this is huge. And Frankie is reveling in every bit of it.

But Jayderay is terrified, her lips forming silent prayers.

RL, face sweating, hand hurting from her grip, his eyes are fixed on the Medium.

And the Bible starts turning in a circle. Slowly.

Jayderay starts a low keening.

The child's voice begins to sing, joined by two others. In a maliciously sing-song, mockingly sweet tone, the children chant.

The Bible turns.

"Daddy loves us this we know, for he does tell us so."

The Bible turns.

"Little ones to him belong, they are weak but daddy is strong."

The Bible turns.

RL tries to release Nostra's hand. He can't. They're as if grown together.

The Bible turns.

"Yes, daddy loves us, and his gate did open wide!"

And then the children laugh in shrill chittering cackles.

The Bible stops.

The laughter fades back into that stretched mouth.

And Frankie screams.

As Nostra crushes his hand, Frankie shrieks while blood spurts from rupturing flesh and snapping bones.

Frankie's fingers break, and the Medium lets go of RL's hand. Slapping his own hand to his face, Nostra digs his fingers in below one eye.

Jayderay slides to the floor, eyes rolling to white, letting go of Frankie. Her other hand still clamped onto RL's.

Frankie's freed hand flies to the straight razor in his back pocket.

"No, no, no! Naughty, naughty, naughty is Mr. Frankie-Wanky," chides the children.

Frankie stops, keeping his hand at that pocket, his face twisting in pain and fear.

"You must not pull the meany, meany razor. We will be ever so crossy cross if you do. We will make Fatty Four By Four roll your poor arm up to the elbow, bony bones and all, just like yummy yum pastry dough. Or we make Fatty Fat do this to you."

Nostra starts pulling at his cheek, the finger nails digging deeper. His meat stretches down, thinning like taffy, the eye above elongating, dripping.

"STOP!" RL yells from his knees beside Jayderay's limp form. "Please, stop. What do you want? Tell us."

Both of Nostra's hands instantly drop to his sides, and he topples forward onto the table. Lying face down, the stretched jaw and chin skewing to one side, tongue lolling out, pulsing. From it, the children sing.

"Reddy Rover, Reddy Rover, you must come over! Play hidey hidey Seek, and you can't peeky peek!"

And it happens.

In the flash of a single second, the Medium and his chair are yanked backwards up the hidden stairs. Arms and head dangling, lower jaw and chin in his lap, he's swallowed by the dark. In a single second.

And the hidden panel slams shut, totally disappearing without a trace.

Dust motes float in the deathly silence, shadows loom, the Bible remains still, and Frankie is the first to speak.

"I'll get you for this, you fat bastard," he hisses toward the invisible panel. And then he whimpers like a little boy, cradling his broken hand.

"How bad is it?" asks RL, still kneeling beside Jayderay.

"From the way it hurts, it's probably mush. What the hell are you doing down on the fl— Jayderay! Is she hurt? I'll get that Pansy son of a—"

"No, she fainted when she heard your bones snap, and I wish I had. We've got to take you to a doctor, Frankie. I'll get Jayderay up, and—"

"I'm not going anywhere, except after that tubby son of a bitch. I've got pain killers and training; you can help me wrap this good enough."

"Frankie, I don't think that poor devil had anything to with this. We asked him here to, to call them, remember. He was just their... their doorway."

"I don't give shit, Boss. He broke my hand, and I'm gonna stuff something up his faggy ass he won't like."

Frankie is lethal. Sweet and lethal. Others have found this out. It was a lasting discovery for them.

"RL… what… what happened? I— Sakes! What am I doin' on the floor? I don't remember any— Frankie! What happened to your hand? Get me up, RL! What you foolin' around down here for? We got to be helpin' him!"

Men often need women to point out little things that they might have otherwise missed. Like Frankie's smashed and bloody hand. Or leaving the toilet seat up, or flushing… or wiping their butt. It's ignoring these little things in life that cause difficulties. As pumpkins need pies to make them something more than just a gourd; men need women to make them something more than… just a gourd.

"Oh, honey, this look bad," Jayderay says, carefully supporting Frankie's arm, as she looks at the hand. "We got to get you to—"

"No!" he interrupts, "I'm going after Flubber Butt; we can fix this hand right here."

"Goin' after him? That devil-man do this, and you want to *find* him? What, you gonna go get the other hand to match? We all just barely escaped bein' toted to hell, and you lookin' for another go round!"

"Yes! I do want another go round, and I'm not—"

"Okay, okay," butts in RL, "I agree with Frankie, we need to go after him pretty quick. Not for revenge, we go because I think we have to. We called the ghosts up, they came, and then they... invited us. They want something. We have to go finish this, or they'll be back, and it won't be for singing."

"You mighty free with that word 'we', white boy. I'm more than afraid of this devilness, RL. And you should be too... both of you!" Jayderay looks fearfully back and forth at the men. "And look like my God still on vacation, he sure didn't help none," she adds, tears in her voice.

"Okay, all right," says Frankie, not wanting Jayderay to start crying. "Let's take a look and see how bad this hand is before we decide anything."

"What! Look and see?" explodes Jayderay, "I'm lookin', and it *look* like it been stepped on by a elephant. A whole herd. And I'm *seein'* a trip to the hospital."

Very soon, that hand will be the least of Frankie's problems. The very least.

RL is right. They have to finish this. If they can.

And there will be graves. Plural.

CHAPTER 7

THAT OLD MAN BELOW

The old man must leave this aquarium region, with its waiting attack-amphibians and those forever-embracing skeletons.

He must continue his search. Not for just a way out, but for a particular one. There is something about a specific door or hatch he cannot yet grasp. But he will know it when he finds it. The man feels this with absolute certainty.

As he exits, the water creatures look on, their orange-ringed eyes glowing softly. When the hatch closes, one immediately shoots away from the glass. The other lingers a few seconds longer, pressing close, studying the door's mechanism with an intelligence that is unmistakable. Then it too slips back into the watery forest of plants.

When the next hibernation shift awakens, they will be told of this reappearance of human. It will matter when they're called to action. And being called is what they exist for.

Remaining in the hatch's entryway, the old man checks the corridor to his right, then left, then upward. The smaller passages have ceilings, but above this main artery, the wall vanish into roiling clouds of fog.

Fragments of the same haze drift constantly at deck level. He assumes it is due to the immense age of the ship. Condensers failing. Purifiers dying by degrees.

He nods, satisfied with himself and the explanation, though he does not know how he evaluated it. He will, the memories will come. He has no doubt.

The pistol tucked into his waistband adds greatly to the man's confidence. Guns have that effect on even the timid and brainless. Perhaps especially on them. But this old fellow is neither timid nor stupid. But what he does not yet know is where, exactly, in this buried starship he walks.

But he is intelligent and has a gun. A deadly combination in any world, so he is confident.

Big hairy deal, old man. A deadly combination? This is the Waydowns. It's a place that eats the smart and armed with the same relish it gnaws on defenseless idiots.

He's about to learn this.

Adjusting his lunch so it rides more comfortably across his shoulders, he steps into the corridor. Cautious, but steadily moving. With the hair leg gripped firmly, hand on pistol, he listens.

Beyond the faint murmurs of long-abandoned workstations and the distant wail of something becoming something's dinner, there is nothing. He continues on.

He passes smaller intersecting hallways and resists the urge to explore them. A way out would be directly off a main corridor, not tucked into some forgotten side channel. At most, what he would find down any of them would be only old, gnawed bones. Or maybe fresh ones, and quite possibly what had done the gnawing.

The man still cannot remember what makes the exit he seeks different from the others, but he trusts the instinct. He will know it when he sees it. He must. The alternative is death, sooner or later. And down here; likely sooner.

Ahead, the passage tees into another. He flips a mental coin and turns left.

The floor slopes, twisting upward almost immediately. Slight at first, then steadily increasing. Before long he is leaning against the wall, sliding along on one shoulder as he walks. He's about to turn back when the corridor begins a sharp curve.

And then it ends. The passage totally ends.

It's not a partial blockage or a collapsed section. It's an absolute ending. No hatches. No openings. No seams. Above, the corridor walls disappear into the ever present, rolling fog. Viewed at this skewed angle does nothing to improve those bilious looking clouds. Even if there were handholds, no one sane would climb up into that.

Like a rat that took the wrong turn in a maze, he studies the dead end. The metal walls and floor flow into one another, smooth and milky, no welds, screws or bolts. The joining is smooth as though melted and poured into a mold.

...Melted... Yes! the experiment... I remember, there was an experiment... it was a disaster and ruined lower parts of the ship... I know this... Many decks were lost, quarantined... I do know this...

The word quarantine sharpens his focus. Total confinement is not applied to measles or chicken pox.

He resists frustration, and knows standing still could be suicidal. It might cause him to end up in a stomach. He turns around, and this lost rat walks back the way it came.

The sloping twist evens out, and familiar debris appears. Rubbish he remembers kicking aside, but now things look different from this direction.

Inside one of the branching halls he spots a door. Not the aquarium hatch, this one is partially open. Which is usual, but something else draws his attention.

A lab coat sleeve dangles from the top edge of the hatch.

He approaches slowly.

The sleeve jerks a bit, and the there's a voice. A woman's voice. Faint. Tremulous.

"Hel... hel me... plee... hel..."

He stops instantly. Draws the pistol. Studies the opening without speaking.

The edges of the door are stained with blood. Old blood. Crusty. The same for the smears on the deck.

Again, the voice sobs, "Plee... plee hel me..."

The old man nods and smiles.

The voice is wrong, it's off. It's trying to sound human, but not totally doing it.

He's never hunted or fished, always considering both the province of little boys. But he understands traps very well. That sleeve is a fishing line, and the voice is a prey-call. An injured animal's cry as lure, but this one is poorly imitated.

Well, this is a two-way street... and both sides can fish.

The chair leg has a barb of metal at one end, still attached from when it was ripped from its frame. Keeping the pistol trained, he reaches out and hooks the sleeve. Then drags it lightly back and forth.

"Plee... plee... hur..."

The sleeve does not move.

... Yes, aren't you a clever shit... you want to see me first... and so you shall...

He slowly twists the still hooked sleeve, giving it more of a grip, and tugs gently.

Something on the other side yanks back hard. And the old man viciously jerks.

The sleeve comes totally free.

And so does the old man.

Falling hard on his rear, his lunch bounces loose, and the pistol skitters across the deck.

And the hatch bursts open.

He was wrong.

It *is* human. Sort of.

And it's a woman. Sort of.

Scrambling, he scoops up the gun and whirls back toward her... but stops.

There is no attack. It's a girl, and she stands blinking, bleary pink eyes darting between the gun and the leg of

Spill. Drool hangs, swaying from her mouth and chin. She points at the flesh, then at herself.

"Hungra... hungra... plee?"

The old man stares.

... she's actually asking...with a please... how provincial. She's not a Spill, yet malformed.

He nods slowly.

She collapses onto the meat, tearing into it with a ripping, gobbling need.

The old man watches, fascinated. He has seen starvation before; a deprivation he had cause. This is a different. This is a need stripped of all pride, and much more enjoyable to see.

He's not worried about sharing his only food.

He has her.

CHAPTER 8

ON NOSTRA'S TRAIL

Frankie's mangled hand is now bandaged, and his arm in a sling. All accomplished with gritted teeth, stifled curses, and Jayderay's gentle help. In addition to Frankie's meds. A lot of Frankie's meds.

RL, doing his part by offering inane suggestions and asking asinine questions, had finally been told to shut up. He had.

This is good training for him, and will be an excellent guide for when he's married.

Frankie, being exceedingly well medicated, has calmed down. Since he's often well medicated without need, this state hasn't changed his overall *Frankieness*. Death might.

"I admit I did... um, uh, I did have to *encourage* Nostra to hold the séance when he got here. Just a weensy bit," says Frankie with a giggle. "He, uh... he was a bit reluctant."

Jayderay an RL glance at one another, remembering the hearse violently rocking as the Medium gyrated maniacally behind its steering wheel. They don't ask.

"So, I guess I do sorta owe it to him to try and get his Pansy ass out of this mess. And like you said, RL, those ghostie girls haven't gone, they invited us, so they're waiting."

"Well," says RL, "Nostra was your idea, *your* Pansy, Frankie. But how are we gonna get up there? While you two were busy with your hand, I looked where that panel was, and I can't even find a joint, much less a switch or a lever."

"He's not *my* Pansy, Boss!"

"Right, so you keep saying."

"But RL, I totally guarantee I can find and open that hidden panel. I've seen dozens and dozens of old movies, and read slathers of mystery books that all have hidden rooms and stairs. You'll see, there'll be a candlestick we pull, or a piece of the banister we twist, or a certain way that—"

The panel slams open.

Cold and dust roll down the stairs.

Webs stir, rustling their dead.

Shadows deepen, getting darker.

Gloom spreads like thoughts from a grave.

The air thickens, curdling like blood.

Lights flicker in ethereal code.

RL and Jayderay clutch each other.

And Frankie giggles.

Of course he does. An intensely medicated Frankie giggles. And cradles his hand.

"If only thunder would boom, and lightning strike something! Man, oh, man, how I do love this house."

"God damn, Frankie, stop it!" snaps RL.

"Okay, okay, Boss. But it's good of the girl ghosties to let us know their invitation still holds." Frankie manages to strangle back another giggle.

"RL, please honey... please... I don't think I can do anymore of this," pleads Jayderay, her fingers clenching the back of his shirt.

"*You're* not, honey. I want you to stay with Shadow, while me and Frankie find Nostra, and see what those things want. She should be able to sense if, if... if they attack us," finishes RL, lamely.

"And then what, RL? Then what?" demands Jayderay. "Yes, they scared of her, but she done said she can't drive'em away. They most killed her man, and they *still* here. Please, don't go, neither of you! We ain't got to move here, we can—"

"I'll buy it, I've got to have this house," dreamily interrupts the medicated wonder. He gazes about soaking up more atmosphere, and adds:

"I'll get all the money from—"

"Oh, shut up... *Dopey*," says RL, running out of patience. "How about you go look in that packing case of Nostra's, maybe there's something in there that'll help."

"Well, don't bother none with that Bible," Jayderay says bitterly. "We just seen how much good that is."

"Okay, I'll have a look, but I doubt if vials of Holy Water filled from the tap, or garlic bulbs sacked in a condom will help much. Maybe I'll— Hey, Boss! Did you just call me Dopey?"

"No, that was earlier, try and keep up."

"Well... does that make you the one called Grumpy?"

"No, Frankie, *you* make me grumpy."

"You both bein' real funny at a bad time," says a frowning Jaderay. "And the first one to call me Snow White gonna get a lot worse than ghosts."

Being the only one of these three with any common sense, Jayderay insists she and RL ask Shadow how to deal with the wraiths.

What an impossible question.

A mother that knows how to deal with daughters?

There ain't no such animal.

———— ✦✦ ————

Still resembling a starvation cadaver, Elvis sleeps while Jaderay and Shadow sit on the edge of his bed. Holding hands, they're both looking at a frustrated RL, who's not getting anywhere with the storm-colored woman.

She's still hurt by their earlier talk, when he inferred that she wasn't human. Such a small thing, just a poor choice of words.

Men are often bewildered when mere innocent words said to a woman land the man… in the shit. Up to his armpits.

And women are smart; they save those words for future reference. Just in case the man forgets. And with almost all women, those words can have an exceedingly long shelf life.

"Need I remind you yet again, RL, I am not as they. I am not dead, therefore I cannot truly know what they want," Shadow says, black eyebrows growing closer together, eyes becoming scary as she continues.

"The magic-man you brought here was too weak, too charlatan; he could only summon, not treat with. They were, and still are, children. They played with him."

"Played with! God damn it, Shadow, they stretched his face like rubber and *crushed* Frankie's hand! I don't call that—"

"Yes, RL, they played!" she almost hisses the words, her scars darkening.

"They might easily have done to him as they did with my Elv-is. Not that he matters overmuch to you, he not being entirely human."

There! Her vocal claws have landed. And the coal black lips tighten, turning down, ready for another verbal swipe.

"Shadow," Jayderay says softly, "I'm lost as why you mad, but please, can you tell us what you... what you feel we might oughta do."

The scarred face softens, and she smiles. "I'm, sorry, my wonderful and true friend. I shouldn't allow myself to be... upset by trifles," she says with a searing glance at RL. "It is of no consequence now," giving him another look. "But I spoke truth to your man. What he asks, is beyond my knowing."

"Well, never mind *him*, he just a man," says Jayderay. "How about you tell me what you can. I know we in bad danger, but how bad?"

"Yes, you... and all beyond this room are in peril. Before this time, my... spawn, came and went on their whims. But your witch-man has called them, they will never go now. Even should I leave this room to confront them. And that I will not do again. I will not leave Elv-is, for I now feel their animosity has increased.”

“Sakes! What do we do, what do they want?”

“If I were to guess, it would be that they long to rest, to cease being, to simply not exist. They chose this path when they died. They had other roads, but they made the choice of wronged children, and they’ve not the ability to undo that.”

“Please, Shadow,” begs RL, unable to keep quiet any longer. “What... what are they going to do? What should we do?”

“Them’s the wrong questions,” Jayderay says, looking steadily at the charcoal hued woman.

“Shadow, *how* are we in danger?”

“I feel it’s *you*, Jayderay. They are focused on you. I was never allowed to be a mother to them, so they feel denied. They’re fixed on you, not to kill... but worse... *to take*. To make you as they are. For you to be their mother in that existence.”

“No,” whispers RL, his face draining to white.

“I, I, I’ll leave. I, I... RL will take me right now,” Jaderay stammers, her eyes swallowing her face. “We can go to—”

“No, my friend, you cannot run from such as they. As long as you are with me, I can and I will protect you. But wherever you might run, they can, and most surely will seek you out. Your only permanent refuge will be to give them the release they long for.”

“How?” demands RL.

“That I do not know. The conjure-man you brought might. If he can be found in time. I sense he still lives, but wishes he did not.”

⸺◆◆⸺

After leaving the women and that slumbering lavender toothpick, RL finds Frankie pawing through the Medium’s trunk. And wearing Nostra’s turban... at quite a jaunty angle. Obviously still quite medicated, and cheerfully so.

“Boss, do you realize we narrowly, teensily escaped having to see brutal nakedness?”

“Jesus, Frankie. What *brutal* nakedness?”

“Well,” he giggles, “if Nostra’s dress had blown off when they snatched him up those steps... the sight of all that nekkidness would’ve sure been brutal.” (giggle)

“Enough bullshit, Frankie! Shadow just told me the wraiths are coming for Jayderay... *they will take her*. It’s her they want. Do you fucking understand?”

Slowly rising from the trunk, taking the turban off, Frankie drops it to the floor.

"I, I, I didn't know that, RL." Fear has replaced the silly bastard's high of moments before. Fear for one of the two people he loves.

"They will not take her, not while I live, Boss. They will not."

"I know they won't, I won't live without her. But we're not up there yet," RL says, shifting his eyes toward the attic. "So, besides playing with that ridiculous turban, did you find anything that might possibly help?"

Stepping to the séance table, Frankie picks up the Bible. Hefting it in his hand, he looks at it, then over at RL.

"This is what we have."

And he walks to the open, dark mouth of those hidden stairs.

"It will be enough," he adds.

The Bible may be enough.

But one of these men... will not.

CHAPTER 9

MEANWHILE, DOWN BELOW

Watching the ravenous female gorge, the old man assesses her. Disdain shows plainly on his face.

It is not disgust at her cannibalism; he acquired a taste for human flesh long ago. Hunger, at least for sustenance, has never been an issue for this man.

He has other appetites. Several of them, and none can be relieved in restaurants. Perhaps in an Asian brothel, where more exotic fare can be purchased. But even those establishments have limits.

This old man has none.

His analysis of the girl is quick and accurate. He's not surprised at this ability, but again, has no idea where it comes from.

...She's definitely not a Spill, but lives with constant hunger. Albinism, worsened by the absence of sunlight. Hair white to transparency, pubic in texture, eyes pink. Signs of dwarfism in overdevelopment of shoulders and

hands. Past facial injuries healed without treatment. Maximum age: twenty. Certainly born here. Raised here.

He watches her intently.

…How has it survived?… There must be others, there is no other way. She has seen firearms., speaks pidgin English… understands to some degree. Has an innate intelligence… Yes… I will use this foul thing. She must know a way out. But will fear it… I must be prepared for that.

Belching, the girl rises and wipes her mouth on the back of a huge hand. She hitches at a ragged loincloth and watches him warily, pale pink eyes never quite leaving the pistol still aimed at her chest.

"Ank oo," she says.

"Well, my, my, such manners you have! You're welcome, my little ugly, twisted ogre," he replies pleasantly. "I'm surprised at gratitude from someone who intended to snare and dine on me. But I graciously accept it."

And he smiles kindly.

But he does not lower the gun. Whoever this old man is, he is not a fool.

She stares blankly, processing tone rather than words. The smile helps. She nods and offers what he interprets as a grin.

Her lower jaw has been smashed some years ago, and had healed on its own, leaving a permanent grimace. It explains the mangled speech and lopsided facial expressions.

Again, he smiles.

And his gun remains steady.

She scratches beneath one arm, then points toward the open hatch.

"Oo come... no go?"

"Why, how generous you are, my dear," he says. "An invitation into your undoubtedly fragrant hovel. Yes. I believe I *should* check whether more of your wretched tribe lurks within."

He smiles, and motions with the pistol.

She pulls on the blood-stained lab coat, covering her small breasts. This is practical, not modest. Intact clothing is hard to come by, and she will need to fish again.

This smiling, kindly old man could tell her that fishing was unlikely to be in her future. Not ever again.

Once inside, the stink is palpable. The area was once a smaller laboratory, long ago wrecked and stripped. And from the stench, whatever space she's chosen as a toilet, does not get cleaned out often. If ever.

She points proudly at a ship distribution tray with attached fountain. It had ceased delivering protein wafers long ago, but the water was huge to the girl.

"Wahr," she announces, as if it were magical and the fountain of life. It certainly is both to her.

Demonstrating with a huge hand, she pushes a button and drinks, then gestures to him.

"Wahr?"

He nods, smiling again. This old man smiles often, each one carrying the benevolence and sincerity of an irritated mosquito.

"Thank you, my dear, I believe I will. And I do appreciate that you didn't place your filthy mouth on the orifice." And of course he smiles.

She understands only thank you, and the smile. And is grateful for both.

He drinks, keeping the gun steady and pointed at her. His lack of memory doesn't equal stupidity.

To this man, trust equals stupidity. As it often does. Everywhere.

She points toward a barricaded corner, where smashed tables, chairs, and assorted trash create a barrier, with more debris piled on top. Within, a pallet of ragged clothes.

"Slee," she says.

"How nice, you're giving me a tour of your rancid quarters," he says pleasantly. "Yes, I'm certain you sleep quite well in there. But I do sincerely hope you are not offering coitus. My penis recoils deep within me at the mere thought."

She searches his face, confused.

He smiles again. And it works again, the girl responding in kind with her twisted mouth.

... *She must know a way out. Or at least a way to the way out. I must try.*

"Way out?" he asks.

And gets nothing. The girl's brow furrows, her eyes searching his face.

"Up?" He asks, pointing.

The pink eyes widen. She shakes her head violently.

"Lers! Lers hungra! Lers ee!"

"So, there is something bad above, bad up?" he says, pointing.

"Ba! she says, nodding emphatically. "Lers hungra!"

"All right, we will try again, my dear. How about... Topside?" he asks pointing upward again.

She grins, her eyes brightening with understanding.

"Op-sigh! No go, op-sigh" she says, shaking her head.

Kneeling, she makes a fist on the deck, raises it slowly, points up, and shakes her head. "No go," she repeats.

The old man's smile is genuine this time.

"An elevator," he murmurs. "You're showing me an elevator! What a clever little pile of feces you are."

For the first time, he puts the gun away. He's getting somewhere.

"Where?" he asks.

Confused, she points up again, and repeats "Op-sigh, no go."

He is patient. He has spoken with primitives before. Some he'd driven into that state, and enjoyed it. He knows this, though not yet why.

With smiles, nods, pantomime and still more tiresome lip stretches, their talk crawls along.

Quite some time passes as he learns and makes assumptions.

She is third-generation. Descended from abandoned staff who survived the mutiny. There are others, but few in number, with rare sightings.

Her parents were taken by a Coiler while in a corridor. Dragged upward by tentacles, screaming, as her father shoved her into a side room before he died. The Lers. The man knows of Coilers, not how, just does.

She has been alone since. She is lonely.

The shared food is enormous to her. Huge. It binds.

Everything this man gleans from her is important.

And he will use it.

After much finger-walking, pointing, and other tiresome gesticulations along with the girl's grunts, nods and head shakes, the old man is satisfied.

She will guide him to the moving room.

To the girl, it is that burned place. Where clean people in whole clothes and guns sometimes come and go. She and her Da had hidden occasionally, watching them. They had even seen those people shoot and kill. She misses her Da, and wishes he could meet this kindly old man.

As she prepares to leave, her reluctance is obvious. This is her home; it has water from the wall. Her Da had found it.

Seeing this, the man increases his smiles of encouragement, and gentle words. Weaponized kindness. He has an endless supply of this.

She retrieves a battered military canteen and a long shard of glass. Placing the glass knife in her coat pocket, she fills the canteen carefully and hangs it around her neck.

"Excellent, my little aromatic dear," he says. "Provisioning is prudent. Even though your chances of return are quite slim." He smiles.

...Faster, you little used tampon. That canteen suggests a longer journey than I'd hoped, so move!

As they leave, she points at the Spill's leg. "Ake?"

"By all means, *ake*." he says, nodding with a smile. "Because of your idiocy, we don't know how long our trek will be, so yes, take it."

Understanding the yes, she grins, hefts the meat, and leads the way.

He follows with pistol in one hand, club in the other. Having been reminded of Coilers, he looks up into the mists often now.

They move quietly through haze and wreckage until she freezes and whispers, "Ba." Pointing with a trembling hand.

Ahead: that yellow glistening growth. The Gunch.

He nods curtly. There is no smile with this nod. Only horror.

Pressed against the opposite corridor wall, they slide past it together. He notes the trapped animal still lives and struggles. Melting slowly.

This abomination of life terrifies the old man each time. He can be frightened, he has been often. It's called having a fucking brain. But seeing this yellow takes him far beyond fright.

It should terrify him. Should he regain his memories, the sight of this yellow thing will become even worse to him.

He will remember it's an extraterrestrial form of a disease whose very name once caused panic on earth. Here in the Waydowns, there is a deck that it has totally consumed. Once-human forms walk on stumps, and try with melting fingers to open the locked hatch. While they could still talk, they had called it The Yellow. Now they are The Yellow.

On that forsaken deck, often one of these desolate yellow creatures can be seen cradling a tool in its arms. Hugging it because there is not enough left of its fingers to grip. Bringing to the hatch workers something that may help in the unlocking. It slides itself along on puddles that were once ankles and feet.

Once the man and girl are a good way past the growth, they breathe easier. And the man's smile is a bit real. But only a bit.

Eventually the corridor opens into a burned section of seared walls and deck. It's not recognizable, but patches of charred Gunch still cling here and there in strips.

The man figures that someone else had known what the growth was. And had firebombed the living shit out of this place. He approves heartily.

Ahead, an elevator door stands, heat blackened. The control panel has been melted, but there is evidence of past repair.

It's still being used.
And memory crashes into the old man.
Total recall, like an avalanche. A tsunami of him.
Not just some, not just a lot, but all. He knows who he is.
He turns to the girl.
He intends to kill her.

CHAPTER 10

UP THE HIDDEN STEPS

Holding the Bible, Frankie walks to the blackness that the panel has revealed.

Those secret steps gradually disappear, rising up into the cold dark. It's a dark caused by more than an absence of light.

It's a dark of oblivion.

It's a swallowing dark.

It's a dark of no return.

And Frankie doesn't give a shit. Jayderay is in danger, and the silly part of this bastard has retired.

This is a man who is no coward. Not when he's silly, and not now. Quite recently he had murdered a large, brutal rapist. Frankie had faced the man with an air of open-faced innocence… just before blinding him with an ice pick. And then castrating him with a straight razor. He had been quite gleeful and innovative about it during the act. And he was man that has no remorse over it. Not even a teensy.

But this is a man who at this moment isn't thinking.

Or he wouldn't have started up the steps.

He's followed by another murderer, RL. A man who at the tender age of ten, had killed his step-father. Had happily sent that strap-wielding turd down to the great commode. Had sent him with a child's hands, and a man's satisfaction.

And he'd felt exactly the same degree of regret as Frankie. There was remorse, however, that he couldn't do the same for his biological father. That drunken asshole who'd christened him Rastus (no middle name) Leroy. Dear old dad had been a diseased penis of a man.

And heading up those steps with Frankie, RL isn't thinking either. What a pair.

These two non-regretting, non-thinking murderers are not going up against monsters or anything human. Nor against anything of this world. In fact, they don't have a dolphin's dick of an idea what they're doing.

They're only idea is to keep Jayderay safe.

That poor woman, she deserves better guards. Ever it is so, good women depending on dipshits.

Fear, like love, can cloud a mind. But thoughts of facing an ethereal unknown can also bring about a miraculous clarity. And then comes the running. This mind cleansing epiphany comes to RL. He's started thinking. Miracles do happen.

"Frankie... just what the devil are we doing?"

"Well, we're going... um, uh... how the hell am I supposed to know, you're the leader... Boss."

"Yeah, a leader that doesn't know shit from a palm tree. Listen, Shadow said that your Pansy is the only one that might be able to release those daughter-ghost things. To get rid of them forever."

"She did? Maybe you need to... he's not *my* Pansy... maybe you need to tell me what she actually said."

"Yes, that way we won't go up those steps without any real plan... like you were about to."

"And here I was thinking you were following, Boss."

A brief silence.

"Well... yes... there is that."

"And what if my Pans— what if Nostra is dead?"

"Well... yes... there is that."

"I'm fortunate to have benefit of your penetrating insight, O Great One."

"Yeah, from shit and a palm tree," sighs RL.

So, these two former murderers and oysters without pearls discuss their options. None are good, and they basically go from bad to worse.

The end result is... that that they go up those steps without a plan. With no idea of what to do.

They chose the worst.

At least now they know it.

Back in the bedroom, Jayderay still sits beside Shadow, trying to hold back the fear, and keep from crying. Neither effort is working well.

"I should be with them. They only goin' on account of me," she says, repeatedly clenching and unclenching her hands.

The gray toned woman places a black nailed hand over Jayderay's, stilling them. And then pats gently.

"Jayderay, your presence would only increase their danger. It is *you* my spawn want. Let the men find and bring down the witch-man. Then we shall see what can be done."

"From what I seen of that fat man, I don't think he have any power over them, Shadow. He just a tea-leaves guesser, and they hexed on him, put him to performing."

"No, you're wrong my friend. They cannot cast spells nor do magic on the living; they are the dead. Through him, they spoke for the first time. Therefore, he does possess some degree of ability; the man is not made entirely of snake oil. He may very well know what it will take to be rid of them."

"Why did they do that to Frankie? Why hurt him if it's me they after?"

"You are a mother figure to him. All can see that plainly. They perceive him as a threat, and have the jealous meanness of all children."

Squeezing Jayderay's hands, she looks at her, worry showing in the scarred face.

"Please, do not take blame when there is none to take. Would you like to kneel with me and pray? We should pray for our friends."

"Oh, Shadow... I wish I had your faith. Mine is all wilty, 'cause it don't never seem like God there anymore, and I feel all stupid on my knees, mumblin' into my hands."

With her ebony lips curving into a gentle smile and dark dimples appearing, Shadow says, "As do I, my friend, as do I. Think of how we must look to God."

"I 'magine we do look a sight, all scrunched up and beggin'," says Jaderay with a mirthless chuckle. "I guess we'd keep Him hoppin' all the time if He let us."

"I am indeed guilty of being a constant asker," says Shadow shaking her head. "Being blessed with child, plus having my Elv-is still recovering, I can't help but call on the Lord to excess."

"Sakes, I been wantin' to ask! How is the baby? You sure not showin' none."

A groan from the bed interrupts as Elvis wakes, struggling to sit up. Grinning his lopsided leer of a smile, greets them both, and reaches for his comb.

Jayderay thinks he must grow hair already coated with Brylcreem. Or hog lard.

In seconds, he whips bed hair into a gleaming duck tail do. Complete with dangling forelock. The original Elvis would be jealous.

That *Do* is the only healthy part of him, the rest is still skin over bone. A 1950s hep-cat skeleton... with stunning hair. Really stunning; it's the color of an eggplant.

Shadow positively beams at him. Love... it's a great filter for reality.

"We were about to speak of our child, Elv-is. And how truly the Lord has shined his blessing upon us." Only the shades of charcoal keep her from glowing like a lit sparkler.

"Yeah, man! Can you dig it, Jayderay? Can you really believe it? I'm gonna be a daddy! I hope it's a girl, and looks just like Shadow."

"Whatever it is, Elv-is, it will be one of God's wonders bestowed upon us, my love. Our Lord will get all the credit and our constant thanks for this miracle."

Jayderay smiles weakly, complimenting them both on their happiness. She owes these people, and deeply cares for them. They're why she made RL buy this place.

But worry crawls through her. She has extreme doubts about this upcoming blessing.

...God might not want no credit for this child. Sakes! What it gonna look like? What it gonna BE? Shadow ain't normal human, and don't nobody know what Elvis is for sure... besides bein' a sorta spaceman from behind the moon. They liable to have to pry the baby off the ceiling just to look... One thing sure, I WILL pray. I will pray for that baby.

———— ◆◆◆ ————

Away from the delighted couple, and the not so delighted Jayderay, two Palm tree guided idiots are ready.

Sort of. Kind of. Maybe.

"When we get up there, remember this house is tricky, we both need to really be on our guard," warns RL.

"I'm ever so glad you're here to tell me important things, O Mighty Oracle. Did that 'be on our guard' nugget come from your mine of wisdom? Or the Palm tree?"

"Okay, okay, but just remember, me and Jaderay got lost once on the second floor looking for your silly ass. Seems like every room had several doors, and none led back to the hall. And we never did find you. I'm telling you, this house is slippery."

"Understood," says Frankie, and he does indeed understand. While they had looked, he had *been with* Shadow. Had really *been with,* and it was a *been with* he can't forget. Or ever talk about.

Slippery house indeed.

Without asking, and pulsing with chemical bravery, Frankie starts toward the steps, taking the lead. RL thinks this is just fine... the boy is the junior partner, let him get boo-ga-booed.

But then he remembers the silly bastard's crushed hand.

"No, let me go first, eager boy. I don't want to get trampled if you have a change of heart."

"That just might happen when we find Nostra, or what's left of him."

"You say the most comforting things. Now, give me the flashlight."

As they climb the dust laden steps, the darkness becomes complete, total. And it feels old, feels thick, feels sluggish. As if undisturbed by light through the passing of long years.

It doesn't want light.

But something higher up does.

The walls on both sides seem to lean inward, exuding a cold that penetrates their bones, going into the marrow. The steps seem endless.

RL's breath rolls out into the flashlight's trembling beam, creating short lived clouds. The illumination does not spread out, and goes no further than a couple of feet, exhausted by the strain.

RL steps onto the attic floor. The air has an indefinable odor. Not just of age, not just of decay, but of despair. Of betrayal. Of treachery.

Of something that wants out.

With the reluctant, subdued light, RL strains to see, spraying the beam around. The darkness is all consuming, and he can make out very little.

"God damn it, RL, I can't see shit through your ankles," hisses Frankie. "Move."

RL edges over... but not forward.

"Jesus, this isn't any better," says Frankie stepping up... but not forward. "Where'd you get that shitty flashlight?" he whispers.

"From you. And I doubt we can keep anything from hearing us by spewing like radiators. They know we're here."

"Yeah, I can sorta feel them listening." Pulling his phone out, Frankie adds to the light... but only a little.

There is enough to get a sense of the room's considerable size, and that it has three doors. Closed doors. But the room itself is empty.

Empty, except for the big something sitting in the middle of it.

"I knew I loved this house," breathes Frankie.

"You won't if Nostra is inside that thing."

The dark listens. And it waits.

CHAPTER 11

THAT MURDEROUS OLD MAN BELOW

The girl stands in the drifting haze, proudly pointing at the fire-blackened elevator door. Her frizzy white hair shines, pink eyes sparkle and crooked mouth grins.

"Op-sigh!" she announces.

And the old man remembers.

It does not come gently. There is no easing-in, no tentative recall. It arrives like a mule's kick to the gut. Sudden, brutal, merciless.

...I... I... I am... Doctor Moto.

He stands frozen, staring at the scorched elevator doors as whole memory floods his brain. Not fragments. Not impressions. Not guessing. Everything. His name, his work, his once high status in the ship... and his current, catastrophic position.

He's in the shit. Deep in it. So deep, tasting is imminent.

This is the dreaded Waydowns. The ship's ruined decks, and laboratory dumping ground. And he's standing beside a half-witted ape girl who has proudly delivered him to the wrong exit.

Yes. Very much the wrong fucking exit.

The elevator before them serves Deck 19.

The deck directly *above* the Waydowns.

The deck from which came the catastrophic screw up that created this horror filled place.

The deck where Doctor Moto once reigned. Second only to Dr. Sally Gaust, whom even God avoided.

During WW2, the honorable Dr. Moto decided the rising sun of Imperial Japan was fizzling into the sea. So, true to his honor... he defected. And swore undying allegiance to the U.S. Government. Exactly as he'd done for Japan.

For decades, Deck 19 had been his kingdom. There he had worked, been revered and created horror and terror in equal measure.

It was also there that Moto had acquired his resistance to ageing, his unnatural longevity. The area he'd spent the majority of time in still emanated the ship's periodic time adjustments. Originally intended for deep space flight, no one but the ship builders knew about this. And they weren't telling, being light-years away.

These time treatments also had mental consequences. Probably the original installers new shit about these. Nor cared, as the results wouldn't be known for a quazillion years or more. And on another planet.

There on Deck 19, Moto had shaped flesh, rewritten DNA, and coaxed monsters into coherence. And there, he had helped design the mutagenic lattice that eventually produced various... *beings*. Not necessarily human ones. There was a lot of practice.

As war raged, the search was on for an Übermensch, a super soldier. The evil Nazis, of course, were accused of doing this. But they were not the only ones playing God.

And Dr. Moto threw himself into that work. With delight.

A side product of his endeavors included the Elvis mutant now recovering in the Roaton house. Which Dr. Moto had been ordered to create. To satisfy the overpowering clitoral itch of his boss, who had a yen for the real Elvis. The mutation hadn't turned out exactly right, being lavender colored. But besides that, it did kind of look like the real thing, sort of maybe. And as it was hung and oversexed... she had made do with it. A lot.

An absolute gully washing torrent of fright runs through Moto's mind:

...No! No, I cannot go back to Deck 19. Up there... I was the Honored Doctor Moto. Up there I was the respected Dr. Moto. Up there I was the feared Dr. Moto.

...But now I would be... the Feces Moto... the Asshole Moto... the Deserter Moto...

He can imagine his return: alarms triggered by biometric scans, old protocols snapping awake like guard dogs. Grunts running. With guns.

And then Dr. Gaust would come.

That Hyena-Vagina Gaust. She of the Elvis itch.

Yes, she would've posted a bounty on him. A very generous one. Live capture preferred. But dead as a can of mackerel quite acceptable. Just as long as Moto's head was intact. That would be a stipulated must, so it could be preserved in jar.

Like the other head she kept on her desk. That one had originally belonged to some Top Brass nose-poker who had plans to shut down Deck 19. He had heard nasty rumors of unsanctioned experiments... on the staff.

Yes, civilian work staff disappearing... with great regularity. Along with alien embryos. Top Brass suspected there just might be a connection. People with brains do occasionally make it to the top. Shocking, but true.

That particular Top Brass brain was never heard from again. But Dr. Moto had seen him regularly. Every time he was called into the Hyena's office... there the bastard was. Or his head was, anyway. In a huge jar of liquid, looking quite lifelike. Too much so. Moto strongly suspected it wasn't dead at all. And got plucked out occasionally for the Hyena's entertainment, and no doubt humorous talks.

...No, I cannot return. I must remain here and be the Wretched Moto, the Diseased Moto, the Fucked Moto... all because this cretinous ape-girl has taken me to the wrong door...

The wretched, the diseased, the fucked Moto turns slowly toward this grinning girl.

He wants to strangle her. He will strangle her. He must strangle her.

The urge blooms bright, hot and immediate. He can feel his fingers closing around her nasty throat, squeezing until those bleary pink eyes pop, and that nasty, snaggle toothed grin collapses forever.

But... he holds it in. Barely. He will satisfy the urge later.

Instead, he summons up that trusty mosquito smile. The smile that has carried him through many decades. It must stretch wearily on.

So, with that kind, stretching of his lips, he looks at her and shakes his head sadly, no.

The girl blinks, confused. She points again, jabbing at the elevator with her oversized hand.

"Op-sigh! Op-sigh!"

Moto shakes his head again. Smile fixed. Jaw aching.

"No," he says again, softly, kindly... wretchedly.

"It is the Wrong Topside, you little porridge brained organism."

She stares at him, brow furrowing. Slowly, uncertainly, she lowers her hand.

"No op-sigh?"

"*Wrong* Topside," he repeats, adding, "Yes, you stupid little collection of polluted genes, you're getting the idea, be it ever so slowly, my dear."

He gestures broadly now, sweeping his arm toward the mist-filled corridors.

"More Topside," he says. "More up."

She watches him carefully. Thinking. Struggling. Wanting to please this kind man who had shared his food.

"Ore op-sigh?" she asks. "Ore up?"

"Yes," Moto says, nodding and smiling. "More up. Very good. More Topside... and I will be pulling your teeth next. Or mine."

He points in several directions, repeating the word, encouraging, patient. His mind screaming frustration behind the smile.

"You've lived in this cesspit your entire vitamin deprived life, you *must* know of another exit."

Reaching beneath her coat, she scratches at her armpit absently, eyes unfocused, trying to understand. Trying to please.

Dr. Moto watches, resisting the urge to apply the chair leg and *assist* her cognition.

"I see you are attempting to think by excavating under your arm," he says pleasantly. "It's about time you tried something, perhaps drooling will also help, my dear."

He smiles wider and points again; away from the elevator.

"More?" he asks.

She glances back toward the blackened doors. Then back to him.

"Ore?"

"Yes," he says quickly. "Yes. More Topside."

Her eyes widen suddenly. She shakes her head, hard and decisively. Both hands wave toward the corridor behind them.

"Way. Way," she says. "Ore way."

Moto's smile becomes almost genuine.

"So," he murmurs softly. "You *do* know of another door."

He studies her closely now, reassessing. Perhaps he won't have to pull teeth. "Is it far?" he asks. "More way?"

She nods vigorously. "Ore way. Ong... ong way."

A distant shriek echoes from above, something hunting, or being hunted. Moto looks up sharply at the open, drifting mists above them. The constant fog concealing whatever moves beyond sight. There are shadowy hints of things writhing up there. Huge things.

Caution first. He gently takes the girl's arm and steers her toward a nearby hatch.

"Come, my dear," he says pleasantly. "Let us discuss this somewhere a bit safer. And then, perhaps, a gentle application of this chair leg will help focus your memories." He smiles.

The girl does know another way. Another exit that leads into... the Roaton house. It is the exit Dr. Moto wants. He has unfinished business there. Painful business, that he will make last.

...Yes, you stupid, malodorous troglodyte. I feel it, this will be the entry I seek. And then I will deal with those who kidnapped me. Those who dumped me into this awful place:

RL, that typical bumbling American. His simpering sidekick boy-girl, Frankie. And Jayderay. Ah, yes... Jayderay, their lovely Negress.

Jayderay will be my dessert. Yes... chocolate cream pie.

CHAPTER 12

BACK IN THE ATTIC

Frankie and RL stand in the dust and cobweb swirled attic room, looking at a large trunk. A very large trunk.

Once again, Frankie proclaims his love for this house.

And RL promptly pees on this emotion.

"Frankie, what if Nostra is in there?"

"There's not a trunk anywhere that could hold that fat ass of his. A shipping container might, but even that would be a tight—"

"That's my point," interrupts RL, continuing "if he's inside that box, he's dead, and we're shafted, because we need him."

"Just what the hell for, Boss? I don't get it. Nostra really messed up the Séance, not to mention my hand, and—"

"No, he didn't screw up the Séance! He called the ghosts, they came, they spoke, and they ended it with a, a, a... summons."

"Yeah, a real cordial summons," says Frankie, glancing at his maimed hand. "Okay, they summoned and we came. So, I ask once again, why is Nostra important now?"

"*And* once again, I will explain," answers RL, running the fingers of one hand through his hair. Twice through, and looking put upon. "It's because Shadow said that your Pansy may understand what they want, what they're asking for, whatever it will take to get rid of them. As long as they're here, Jayderay is in danger, even if she leaves this house. We've got to find him, Frankie."

"Well, they... he's not mine... they were in the bastard's mouth, why didn't they just tell us?" says Frankie, looking at his hand some more.

"Do I look like I'm one of the dead? How would I know?"

"Well, Boss, you do always look kinda bad, but I get your drift. What if we can open this thing, and he's in there, then he'll have to be dead and *he* can tell us."

"Jesus, Frankie! After that séance, if we open it and a squashed dead man has been stuffed in there and he *squeaks* at us, this would all be over... 'cause we'd shit ourselves to death."

With a few strained giggles, Frankie nods, saying, "I hadn't thought that far. But we do need to know if... well... if he's inside it. Don't we?"

He also really, really wants to see inside that chest. He just absolutely knows it will be something Haunted House Wonderful. Of course, Frankie is still well medicated. And he's partly wrong about the chest. The wonderful part.

Spots of rust cover the rectangular, iron banded trunk. There are no handles, yet it's huge, especially for an iron chest. It would be onerously heavy, even when empty.

A big man's body could probably be stuffed in this trunk… after some judicious whittling. And if the corpulent Medium is inside, he has indeed been whittled. Or worse. He could've been rendered down and poured in. In this house, that is a possibility. Likely, even.

"Yeah, I guess we do have to find out," answers RL, kneeling down beside the metal box. "Well, of course there's no damn lock or keyhole showing on this bastard. You don't suppose this is the bottom, do you?"

"It does kinda look like the seam could be in the middle of two halves, so maybe it's like upside down. See if you can flip it over, I can't help with this busted hand."

After pushing and pulling on a corner of the trunk, and then trying again on the opposite end, RL gives Frankie a disgusted look.

"This son of a bitch would give a hernia to Superman. I don't see how this old floor even supports it. If your Pansy is in there, he better have a can opener with him. And I'm not sure there is any seam anywhere."

"He's not my— oh, fuck it. It's got to have a seam, Boss. There has to be a way to open it."

"No, not in this house there doesn't. In case you haven't noticed, nothing in this place is right," RL snorts in disgust as he stands. "I don't think there is a seam, there is no way to open it."

Frankie giggles and says, "I got a bad feeling about this. You know, like they're always sayin' in Star Wars."

"Yeah, but that's movie, it didn't have a trunk, and it had a good ending. This is no film, and we may not."

"You're so cheery. Okay, then screw the trunk, we pretty much know he's not in there anyway. So, what do we do? This standing around in the cold is making my hand throb."

"I've been throbbing since that panel flew open, Frankie. Not with cold either, I'm scared."

"Get a grip, Boss. I'm beginning to think this is just old movie haunted house stuff. It'll work out, you'll see. But we do have to do something... *Noble Leader of mine.*"

"Yeah, running like hell comes to mind. Okay, eager boy, there's these three doors we haven't tried yet. And

I admit, I'm not real hot on the idea of opening any of them."

"Yeah, it is kinda like that old 'what's behind the door' story. You know, it's either a tiger or a girl... and you figure we'll probably get a tiger, right?"

"I'd kiss the tiger's butt and thank it, Frankie. It's probably gonna be one of those wraith things... there's three of them, and three doors. I don't think that's a co-incidence."

"Christ, RL. You're such a comfort. You make that trunk sound like just a big Easter egg."

"Eggs can be rotten and have dead things inside, you know."

"Okay, that does it, you happy asshole. You're the leader, RL, so lead... let's do *something*."

RL does exactly that.

Lunging forward without speaking, he yanks open the nearest door. Frankie squawks, as the cold, lonely air of long ago spirals out into the weak light.

"Goddamn it, Boss! You could've warned me, I, I..." Frankie trails off into rare silence, staring into the opening.

"You did say to do something, Frankie."

"True... I did," he answers, gazing rapturously through the opened door.

"And yes, to what you're thinking, RL. I do totally, totally, absolutely love this house."

A few feet beyond the newly opened door, lays a skeleton. From the size, it appears male. Clad in the tattered remnants of work khakis, both arms stretched toward the opening. As if the former owner of the bones had been running, desperately trying to escape something.

He hadn't made it.

"One thing we do know," says RL, pointing with the flashlight, "*that* sure as hell ain't Nostra."

"Well, it might be, you know they've got some raging good diet pills these days," giggles Frankie.

"Then I'd say he's had enough," replies RL, taking a couple steps through the opening, looking down at the bones.

"This is so, so haunted house shit, Boss! Every book, every movie... there's always a skeleton. And I'll bet that reeely mysterious trunk has treasure in it. Damn, I just love this house."

"Oh, do shut up," says RL with a long sigh, shaking his head. "So, who is this bastard? Looks like he's got some type of tool belt on and is in work clothes... maybe some kind of repairman? I can well believe one could get lost working in this place, but how'd he windup in the attic? It's not exactly easy to find."

"Boss... uh, maybe he was, you know, *shown how*... like we were."

"Jesus. If that's so, then it would mean—"

"No, wait a minute," interrupts Frankie, "that's not it. Elvis has told me that back in that buried spaceship where he was hatched, they had some full-time repairmen. And sometimes they'd get sent into maintenance tunnels and never make it out. Bonesy here could be one of them."

"Maybe," replies RL, nodding. "But still, how did he get from the ship into the house?"

"Well... Elvis did. And you and me went into it through that breastplate/portal thing, snatched Moto, and brought that shithook back."

"Yeah, you're right, I guess that's more likely where this guy came from... oh, hell, Frankie! Why are we even talking about this? It doesn't matter who it is, or how he got here."

"No, not really," giggles Frankie. "It's not like we can be good citizens and report it to the police."

"Good citizens, your giggling ass... good citizens land in jail. Can you just imagine this as a crime scene? And here we are... with Nostra's 'Having Fun With Death' vehicle parked in front, and him missing."

"Oh, yeah, and of course the law *would* find him. Probably with a mattress stuffed up his dead butt (giggle) or something that could actually fill it. (giggle) There wouldn't be any explaining—"

"FRANKIE!" shrieks RL. "What is that?" pointing his shaking flashlight further into the room.

While the two men had talked about their skeletal find, the dust had settled. Settled a lot... settled way too much.

Their lights now reveal a large hole in the floor. Almost four foot in diameter, where something has pulled the wood flooring downward into a twisting funnel that curves into a dark hole. A big, dark, awful hole.

At the floor opening, a sick looking white substance coats the rim, and strings of it make ladders swirling on down into the dark. Thick strands for climbing.

It's nothing any human would ever want to touch.

The surface of that downward spiraling tunnel is coated with it.

It's a web.

A web with threads as thick as rope. One strand twitches, jerking, briefly yanked from below. Neither man sees this.

Creeping closer, RL and Frankie spray their lights over the slightly shimmering webbed funnel.

"Boss, is that what I think it is?" Frankie asks, looking at the hole.

"In this house... of course it is. And I just hate spiders. Big time."

"Usually I'm not afraid of them, but this is, um... is definitely not one of those times. RL... it must be enormous... have you ever heard of an Australian Funnel Spider?"

Behind them, the skeleton silently rolls onto its back.

"No, Frankie, and I don't want to. Spiders aren't exactly my favorite subject."

The skeleton raises its skull from the floor. Empty black holes stare at the backs of the two men.

"Christ, Boss... it, it *smashed and pulled* the floor down into a cone."

"Yeah, yeah, I can see that. Thanks so much for pointing it out."

"Under the circumstances RL, I think you better hear about a funnel spider."

The skeleton sits up, its teeth gleaming a rictus smile. Bits of dried scalp with hair shower onto the shoulders.

The name stitched to its khaki shirt reads: Gary.

"No, Frankie! I'm not listening to any crap about things with a lot of legs. And since you're so eager to tell, I'm sure the Australian bastard eats shop owners."

And behind the web-entranced men... are moving bones. Slow. Silent. Secret.

The skeleton rises.

CHAPTER 13

KINDLY DR. MOTO AND THE GIRL

This long-buried starship crashed into Earth many hundreds of thousands of years ago. Other than barbecuing a few dinosaurs, it had little effect on the planet. Earth peacefully went back to sleep for a very long time.

But then something struggled up out of the mud that had nothing to do with the wrecked ship.

It was God's accident: that cursed contaminant.

Eventually, this muddy something began crawling about and making noises. Fairly soon after that, the noisy crawler evolved into an upright, perpetually destructive pain in the ass.

Humanity had arrived. And began... begatting.

This ended all peace on Earth. It would certainly be of no comfort to the Deity either.

Present-day examples of that insufficiently evolved, upright contaminant are everywhere on Earth.

Even here, in the bowels of this ancient UFO, there is a prime example: Moto.

Before being kidnapped from Deck 19 and yanked into the Roaton House, Doctor Moto had once been hot shit.

A much feared and deadly member of Deck 19's command structure. Now he was just cold doo-doo… and in the Waydowns. And with an odorific girl he despised, yet must coddle along. Baby and coax her if he was ever to find a way back into the Roaton House.

After that, he intended to lovingly beat her into a squalling pulp. He keeps the chair leg handy.

As the girl admits that she *does* know of another doorway to Topside, Moto sighs with relief.

"So, my little putrid pile, you know of another entrance," he states in his kind, friendly voice. And smiles.

Glancing up into the roiling, bruise-colored murk above them, he adds, "First, let us move to a place with a ceiling. We mustn't have those dreadful 'Lers' dropping down on us."

With pink eyes widening and her head shaking no, she said, "Lers ba. Lers ba, ake Da!"

"Yes, my dear, they are bad. No doubt you mean Coilers, which I've heard about from the ship grunts," he says, pointing as they walked across the corridor toward an open hatchway.

Nodding, she follows the kindly old man. And the kindly old man conversationally tells her how he'd love to give her nasty ass to the Lers. There were benefits to this girl-ape not understanding many of his words.

Dr. Moto was indeed a foul piece of work. He had been since birth. It has served him well. And many of his *tastes* had been altered by being in a certain area of the ship. He did not practice any of these tastes or needs with anyone who would tell. There was no worry; none survived.

Yes, Moto had it made on Deck 19, until those two round-eyes, RL and Frankie, kidnapped him from the ship. At gunpoint. How rude. And after using him horribly, they had tossed his honorable ass into the Waydowns.

How rude-er.

Cautiously entering a room, both man and girl make sure there is a ceiling, then do a brief check of the area. Surprises in the Waydowns were seldom pleasant and often involved getting eaten... during the dying process.

But they found only the perpetually drifting haze, blinking lights from long-deserted terminals, and more broken equipment.

Assuming his benign, oriental smiley face, Moto turns to her.

"Now, my little smashed-jaw beauty, you've said you know of more Topside, and that it's a long way."

She starts shaking her head. "Ore Op-sigh, ong—"

"Yes, yes, yes," interrupts the smiling face. "There's no need to repeat. No need to send more of your gut breath wafting about. It is a long way, yes, yes."

And he smiles of course, nodding. Kindly.

"Let us try some more silent communication."

Pointing at himself, then at her, he finger-walked across his hand, saying, "More Topside." He repeated this a couple more times.

The pink eyes watched these performances intently. Then her shoulders slumped, and she looked down at the trash on the deck, pushing pieces around with a grimy foot. The toenails resemble badly abused chisels.

Slowly raising her head, looking truly apologetic, she removes the Spill's leg from around her neck and places it at his feet. Stepping back, she shook her head, no.

She feels badly about refusing this kindly man who had shared his food, but she has repaid him. She had taken him to the door to Topside, as he had wanted. What he asks now was just too, too far away.

She is afraid to leave her home for such a long, dangerous trip. Her place has water from the wall. Her Da had found it. Something might move in.

That kind, smiley face of the good Dr. Moto doesn't slip. Doesn't change. It is a very high-mileage smile.

He well knows the girl could quite easily be forced. He has a gun, and she knows what it is.

And he could also knock her out with the chair leg, break both arms, and then repeatedly insert it rectally until she regained consciousness.

The latter holds great allure for the kindly Moto. The honorable doctor has needs.

But from much past and bitter experience, Moto knew that information gotten through torture couldn't be trusted.

The group of American POWs he'd been given during the early part of WW2 had taught him that. Those foul, lying tricksters. They had badly misled him. And they had paid.

...This filthy swine-girl would be no different than those sniveling, weak Americans I experimented on... What monstrous lies they told me... She would lie, get me lost, abandon me. No, I must have her willing cooperation. I must restrain myself from bestowing a justly deserved reaming...

...Besides, it would make her walk slower.

So, Moto's kindly, gentle smile stays in place. But now it is visibly tinged with sadness. A little hurt-looking. The poor, poor old fellow.

"I see, my dear," he says sorrowfully. "Well then, how about some inducements even your monkey brain can relate to? Perhaps greed will sway you. Avarice is universal—even among brainless primitives such as you."

Feeling that she has hurt the kindly old man, the girl frowns, trying hard to understand his words.

He nudged the Spill meat lying on the deck. "More? Much more?" Pointing at the meat, he made a sweeping gesture taking in the whole room, repeating the word.

She stood watching, blinking, her face twisting in confusion.

Moto pointed to her canteen. "Want more? Much more?" He mimed water levels rising up a wall.

But she already has that water fountain, so he goes back to promising meat. There's more pointing at the leg, more imitations of mountains. And on. And smiling. Always smiling.

The girl tries hard, concentrating, pink eyes narrowed, one oversized hand scratching at the white, wiry hair.

"Yes, my dear," Moto murmurs, "no doubt stirring your wool will warm up that flaccid brain." He stretched his lips reassuringly... and thinks longingly of lip balm.

And he continues to be patient. Knowing that he has no choice but to continue this nice act, gnaws viciously at his innards. But he must endure. He doesn't feel sorry for himself; self-pity is for the weak. But he will make the girl pay, and that will be quite rewarding.

He runs through several more gesticulated variations of how helping this kindly old fellow will benefit her.

He smiles a lot. He nods encouragingly. A lot. And he silently curses. A lot.

During one of his descriptive gyrations, the girl's pink eyes suddenly grow wide.

"Ore?" she exclaims, pointing at the Spill flesh. "Ore?" she asks again, jabbing the big hand once more at the meat. Then, with a questioning look, she jabs a thick thumb to her chest.

Moto nods like a jackhammer. Moto smiles so big his face is an O.

Moto is a cold-blooded, ulcerated dick head, but at this moment, a sincerely happy one.

"Very good, my little dimwitted Neanderthal! At last, we've awakened some synapses beneath that sloping bone that's supposed to be a skull. Yes—more for you!

More for you," he says pointing at the girl. "Yes, yes, yes, *MORE!*" continues the kind old Moto.

"Positively rooms full of more," he gushes like a car salesman. "All for you, little toilet mouth." And on he goes, nodding maniacally.

There were additional rounds of finger-walking and arm-waving, answered by grunts of "Ba!" and head shakes or nods with crude hand gestures.

The word *Ba!* predominates.

This is the Waydowns, where everything is indeed... "Ba."

Eventually, they leave the relative safety of this room with a ceiling. Moto has persevered. And fully expects to make this stupid girl pay for being so ignorant. But first things first; use her. Use her up.

The girl does understand what is wanted of her. And she's fearful of the things they may run into, but the kind man does have a gun. He will protect her.

She goes with visions of meat enough to fill rooms and last forever.

Dr. Moto also goes with visions.

His revolve around those two round-eye twerps in the Roaton House. And their black woman. Moto seethes thinking about them holding him captive. And it was all done for the benefit of an Elvis mutant who was no better than a Lab Spill. Or this crusty fatuous thing leading him. And the doctor feels that it's all just so... unjust.

Out in the corridor again, passing more dangling strips of fire-blackened Gunch, Moto keeps an eye on the churning mists above. He noticed the girl had picked the Spill's leg back up and draped it around her neck.

Hunger has never been far away from this girl, so Moto is sure his promise of a mountain of meat will keep her in line. Greed is powerful at securing loyalty and co-operation.

And there is the chair leg, should she falter.

He keeps looking up, knowing that what might drop down from those bruised-looking clouds above... would make Moto the meat.

It was the looking up that got Dr. Moto in trouble.

And in the Waydowns, trouble means death.

Or worse.

CHAPTER 14

BONES AT THE ROATON HOUSE

As they gaze down into that web-coated swirl of a funnel, RL tries desperately to keep Frankie from telling him about spiders. Any kind of spider.

"No! I'm not gonna listen to any more of your shit about... about... *this*," says RL, pointing at the awful web hole.

"But, Boss, you really need to hear—"

Like a released breath, a sudden gust of air from the opening interrupts him, making the web strands move and shimmer. The smell is dank, foul and frightening.

Three of those thick strings of web jerk down slightly, then spring back into place, quivering in the weak light.

"Did you see that? God damn it, Frankie, we woke the bastard!"

And behind them, the skeleton begins to slowly stand.

"RL, I bet the thing never sleeps, I... I don't think spiders do."

"Oh, thanks a lot, you... you shit."

The skeleton's moldering work belt slips, falling to the floor with a deadly thud and a clanking of tools.

Both men let out squeaky versions of "Eeyah!" as they spin toward the sound.

They do not quite leap into each other's arms, but are suddenly much closer together. They're also stuck between the gaping maw of a giant spider's den and a clanking representative of the dead.

They are exceedingly aware of this.

The skeleton turns its head slightly back and forth as pieces of scalp and hair fall to its shoulders. The skull's empty sockets stare blackly at each man in turn. The teeth display that forever smile of the fleshless.

And Frankie... giggles. Of course he does. He's medicated and he's Frankie.

"Don't worry, Boss. This is bullshit."

"Bullshit? Like hell it is. It's as real as we are, and the name tag on its shirt," answers RL. "Hell, it's even got dandruff."

"Yeah, looks like maybe he died from it. Death by dandruff. (giggle) Look, Boss, the bones are real, but this moving around isn't. I've seen plenty enough movies to know. This sack of bonemeal won't really do anything.

It's just those ghostie girls screwin' with us. It'll probably take a step, flap its jaws, and then fall to pieces."

"And that'll be plenty enough, Frankie. I'm already about to piss my—"

The skeleton interrupts him with a step forward, right on cue. One rotten work boot splits open at the sole.

Tiny bones spill out into the dust, tumbling like deformed dice.

"See? I told you, RL. He's already coming apart."

"I wasn't worried about his fucking toes."

The skeleton's jaws open. RL moans.

The other foot raises and slams down, dust spewing out from beneath it. The jaws snap shut with audible clacking force, spraying chips of teeth.

They open again. Wider.

"I'm ready for that 'falling to pieces' part, Frankie."

"Any minute now, Boss. Don't be so fidgety."

"Fidgety's ass! It's nearly here, and there's a spider's trap behind us!"

The jaws snap shut again with the sound of breaking teeth. Enamel chips fall, sprinkling the ancient shirt, dusting the name Gary.

"Christ, Frankie!"

The bones of the other leg lift for yet another step.

And the foot crashes down. The second boot splits open. The wooden floor shakes, and the sick-white web ripples from the vibrations.

"You're making me look bad, you clattering bastard," Frankie says, sounding worried for the first time. "You're losing the plot, *Gary*... collapse, you asshole!"

The jaws open again; the cracked and splintered teeth form a jagged cave.

As Frankie realizes his movie lore has failed him, RL raises the flashlight like a club.

The advancing Gary is nothing compared to what may lurk down that funnel-shaped web. RL plans on breaking that bony head, stomping over him, and running like hell. Let Frankie deal with the spider.

Starting to sway, the skeleton turns its head back and forth repeatedly, as if trying to tell someone no. The swaying grows worse. It is less than a yard away.

"Finally," breathes Frankie. "He's about to fall apart."

The skeleton's wavering becomes circular, rotating, and more dried scalp flies loose.

"Are you gonna dandruff us to death? Go to pieces, you bony son of a bitch!" yells Frankie.

Abruptly, the skeleton throws its arms wide open, jaws agape.

And leaps directly for RL.

Frankie shrieks. RL does not.

Time does not fiddle around at moments like these. There is no stretching, no slow-motion nonsense. Hell just blossoms and the shit flows.

The skeleton's forward lunge hits RL full-on, carrying them both over the edge into the web-coated funnel. As they roll and spiral downward, the skeleton comes apart, sending rotten pants, shirt, and bones in all directions.

Clutching desperately, RL finds only webs and chunks of wrecked flooring to grab. Nothing stops his fall. The dropped flashlight rolls away from him, casting a Ferris wheel of spinning light.

Frankie watches in frozen horror as RL disappears silently into the hole. The skeleton's pieces snag here and there in the foul stickiness. The skull rolls until it catches on the rim, as the funnel's darkness stretches on down to what built it.

The flashlight, wedged in twisted floorboards, illuminates the white skull against the blackness. The eye sockets stare lifelessly up at Frankie. It is now as dead as it should be.

Its mission is complete, and this is no Disney movie.

Sinking to his knees in the cold dark room, Frankie stares into the blackness with disbelieving loss and horror. He hugs himself, because there is no one else. His hand throbs.

With the voice of a terrified, abandoned little boy, he shouts:

"RL? Please... RL? Don't you leave me. I can't do this alone. RL... what about Jayderay? Why didn't you scream? You come back, damn you!"

A fetid draft of air blows briefly from the abyss. The webs ripple and shine in the weak light.

It's an exhalation.

And it is the only response Frankie gets. The silence breaks his heart.

⎯⎯ ◆ ◆ ⎯⎯

Downstairs, the recovering Elvis dozes fitfully. Jayderay and Shadow sit at the foot of his bed, chatting. By unspoken agreement, they avoid the subject of where the two fools have gone.

But the topic fills the room anyway.

Like a constipated green elephant.

No one can chat and visit like women who truly like each other can. This chatting part is not rare; women can do that with great ease. But the *liking* part, however, is quite rare. Most women do not like most women. They find them untrustworthy.

Imagine that. How shocking.

Perhaps for these two, the liking has something to do with both being women of color, if gray and creamed coffee could be considered colors. Plus... one of them is not exactly, not precisely, not entirely human.

She is kinda, sorta... part house.

Part *this* house.

A wrong house absorbed a wronged woman long ago, and neither was ever the same. Women profoundly affect everything. Usually to the better: just look at married men. In this case, the house became somewhat less lethal. It left that to Shadow. She was more than capable.

"Shadow, you bein' with child is no time to be lifting anything heavy," Jayderay says, looking pointedly at the sleeping Elvis.

The ebony lips of this storm gray woman smile gently, as one black eyebrow arches.

"Yes, my true friend. And I accept your concern with gratitude. But my Elv-is is not heavy to me, and I have had some small experience with pregnancy."

"Oh, sakes, of course you have," Jayderay chuckles. "I most forgot about your... uh... the... um, your daughters."

With a sharp intake of breath, Shadow reaches out, gripping Jayderay's hand.

"He screamed," she whispers. "RL screamed."

Elvis jerks upright, eyes darting. "Baby! I just heard... I... was that Mr. RL?"

Bewildered, Jayderay looks between them. Fear crawls across her face.

"I don't hear nothing. You both heard RL? He in danger? I gotta get to him, I gotta go!"

"NO!" Shadow says, tightening her grip. "It is *you* they want. You must not go. There could be no return."

Abruptly, Elvis swings his spindly legs off the bed.

"Well, *I* am going. Mr. RL would go if it was me," he says, trying to stand. His knees buckle.

As Shadow lunges to catch him, Jayderay wrenches free.

The heart is a beast. It will shred the brain into gruel. And the body will follow the heart.

Running for the door, Jayderay knows she can do nothing but make things worse. But she is going. She will follow her heart, there is no choice.

Love is indeed a wondrous thing. An earthbound hint of heaven.

But it can kill.

And it can be killed.

———— ✦ ————

At this same moment in town, Princess jumps out of her sleep. Howling, she begins running in circles, snapping at the air. Bumping into furniture, bawling out whining barks, her eyes showing white, tail tucked tightly between her legs. Urine seeps down her haunches, the fur wet with it. Three times the dog bays at the ceiling in anguish.

In the house next door, George bolts upright on the desk, his fur standing out as if electrified. Golden eyes bright, glowing feral, bulging, as a low growling comes from deep in the cat's chest. He lets out a spitting hiss, aimed at something only he sees. George does this three times.

———◆◆◆———

Back in the attic, kneeling at the funnel's edge, Frankie sobs, wiping at his nose and eyes. Taking a deep, shuddering breath, he begins to climb down into the web. Love is brave... especially when the heart has shredded reason.

His maimed hand screams as he puts weight on it. The thick webs cling, burning. He yanks it back. Red welts mark where the strands had touched him. Pulling back, kneeling at the edge of this abyss, the little boy cries into his hands.

He cannot do this; his body will not allow it. And he knows it. And realizes it would not help even if he could. Whatever has taken RL, it will take more than a gay shopkeeper to rescue him. Even a lethal one like Frankie.

... I can't, RL... I can't... why didn't you scream?... are you...are you dead? Don't... don't you die on me... Think of Jayderay, RL... you can't be dead...

And then they came.

CHAPTER 15

MEANWHILE, IN THE WAYDOWNS

As the girl leads Moto down the trash littered, white corridor, he continues to look upward often.

This is prudent. The constantly moving vapors above this passageway hide things. Terrible, living things... things that have no dietary restraints. A troll of a girl, or an aged scientist, would be consumed with equally delighted appreciation. Lip smacking likely. Provided they have any lips... this is the Waydowns, not Mc Donalds.

Having bought the girl's loyalty with his promise of food without limit, Dr. Moto isn't overly worried about where she's leading. It's not about trust, only fools trust, and this Doctor is far too smart for that. But the girl knows the way, and wants the grub. The food will bind her.

And besides, the crooked faced little idiot is the one in front. Yes, Moto is smart. But even the most intelligent of buttholes can screw up. And Dr. Moto will.

Ahead, foul danger crawls toward them. Where the deck meets a corridor wall, it moves along with deceptive speed. All eight feet of it are advancing remarkably well for something with so many legs. Hundreds of red tipped, black legs, carry a blacker body with the girth of a huge melon.

It pauses, slowly lifting its head, legs waving. The head is the size of a beachball, yet there are no discernable eyes. It does quite well without them.

And Moto is looking up, worried about Coilers, and walking.

Grunting as she spots the creature, the girl immediately backs into the upward looking Moto.

He sees what she sees, and also grunts. And loses all interest in cloud-gazing.

"Eeed," says the girl softly, clutching her glass shard, "Ba." Shaking her head, as she pushes the old man further back. Turning slightly toward him, she points to the gun tucked in his waist band, and then at the black segmented creature. "Eeed," she says again.

Frowning, Moto doesn't speak, but quietly studies the creature a few seconds. He knows even at this close range, hitting it with a pistol shot would be luck. The things head is the only possible killing spot and while big, not big enough for a sure hit.

... Bullets are precious and the noise of gunshots could attract things even worse, I must wait till it's closer, or perhaps evade it by...

As if on cue, the head raises further, swiveling toward them, as bright red pincers extend. They open and close repeatedly, their tips dripping fluid. It chitters. A noise both hungry and menacing. It is decidedly not a vegetarian.

Again, the girl frantically points at Moto's pistol, her eyes huge and terrified. The old man must act, must use the gun.

The head rises further; it's upper body now over three feet off the floor. The suspended part starts swaying, as the head continues to swivel, the legs waving in the air. It's searching for them.

Grunting indecipherable words, the girl implores him to use the gun. Her gibberish is the equivalent of: "Quit fucking around! Shoot!"

Still watching, Moto reaches out and places his hand across the girl's mouth, as he thinks.

... it's blind. It sees by sound vibrations or odor detection. This putrid girl's stench has probably attracted it. My own knees may buckle soon from her reek. If I didn't need her, I'd shove this smelly, stupid twat into the creature.

The head stops turning, pointing directly at them. The body stills, then slowly lowers to the deck.

Blind or not, it has pinpointed their location.

It chitters, as countless feet make a dry, deadly sound, moving forward.

Drawing the pistol with one hand, Moto takes the other away from the girl's mouth. She understands not to make a sound. The man will shoot the Eeed, and save them both.

The thing comes slowly toward them, head fixed.

Finally, Moto points the gun, while protectively placing an arm around her shoulders. He tenses that protective arm.

The arm is protective; it's greatly protecting Moto. Should he miss... into to the creature she goes.

...that will save me, but then the Honorable Dr. Moto will be lost, and most honorably fucked... I must risk the noise of gunfire...

The monster speeds up, its legs becoming a blur.

Moto shoots, but the gun does not fire.

And Moto uses that protective arm to snatch the Spill leg from the girl's shoulders, slinging it at the creature's head.

Both man and girl run... like a fucking monster was after them.

The thing catches the meat, burrowing pinchers deep into flesh. Its upper body attaches itself the full length of the prize, the poison tipped legs digging in. The lower segments of the creature carry it and the bloody leg away.

Reaching a turn in the corridor, Moto risks a look back and finds the Eeed has disappeared.

Leaning back against the wall in relief and from lack of oxygen, he nods to the girl.

"It's gone," he pants, scowling at the gun in his hand.

This is the Waydowns, where Murphy's law is richly smeared on everything. Like troweled shit. The pistol had been down here when that long ago catastrophe hit. It could well be altered. He had checked it when found, but only a quick once over.

Moto is pragmatic, and doesn't toss it away in disgust, he will dismantle and clean. It will fire after that. Or explode. He may have the girl fire a round, under the guise of teaching her. While smiling and nodding, of course.

But not right now. Not standing here in a corridor with Coilers probably peering down. And he needs to keep the girl moving. He figures her greedy commitment concerning the promised mountain of meat could become slippery.

Especially when faced with Eeeds and other minor forms of being eaten alive.

"No doubt my brilliant move with the Spill's haunch has saved us, my little toilet. It was probably your abominable odor that attracted it, but I'll excuse that for now."

Not understanding any of what the old man said, but realizing the danger has past, the girl reaches timidly for his hand. Kneeling, she looks up.

"Ank oo."

"Yes, yes, gratitude. How charming. And indeed, you should be grateful, but I've no time for cave-style fawning." He stretches his lips again into the benign mosquito smile, nodding as he pulls her up.

"Now my dear, we must continue on to the More Topside," Moto says, pushing her forward firmly, and adds, "Move along, lest I encourage you in a manner you would consider less than desirable. I would indeed find the act quite pleasurable, but that's beside the point. Perhaps... even probably, I will attend to that later."

They walk on through the patches of drifting fog, passing discarded trash and open hatches revealing more of the same. In some areas, the blinking of ancient warning lights still flash redly.

Those lights have flashed in vain. When they began their silent warning, the holocaust's molecule twirling was already complete. It had happened in a second. And then the results had begun, and for decades they have continued. And the lights kept on blinking, cautioning the walking dead of the Waydowns.

Coming to yet another corridor branch in this melded, twisted world, the girl stops, frowning. Looking about, shaking her head, obviously confused.

"Have you exhausted your anemic brain cells?" asks the perpetually smiling Moto. "I'm really growing tired of all this, and my restraint from inserting the chair leg into you weakens."

As the girl continues to study the branching hall, he sighs. Giving her a disgusted look, he walks impatiently past her, and turns a corner.

Turning a corner without caution in the Waydowns is exceedingly injudicious. Also known as really fucking up.

Moto just has.

Badly.

CHAPTER # 16

LOSS AT THE ROATON HOUSE

On his knees at the edge of the web's opening, Frankie's back heaves with sobbing. There is no silly bastard left, nor any brave man. There is only a hollow little boy who is totally devastated by loss. Gutted by his own cowardice.

RL is the only real friend Frankie has ever had, and now this accursed house has taken him. Taken him into that dark hole at the bottom of this web-smeared funnel.

And the man had fallen silently into the abyss.

Fell silently. Deadly silent. No shrieks of terror, no screams, no shouted pleas for help. Just that horrible, tumbling, spinning spiral down. And then gone into blackness.

"Don't you die on me, RL, you, you, oh... God damn you! Don't you be dead." Frankie screeches. "I'm gonna go, I'll get Shadow, she'll know what to—"

And then they came.

Starting with a gust from the abyss that interrupts him. Web strands stir, blowing outward. The skull rocks in the wedged flashlight's beam, its empty eye sockets stare accusingly at Frankie. Sending a silent message:

Your fault. You told him it was all only movie crap. Your fault. You told him it was not real. Your fault he did not run in time. Your fault... your fault...

Dank air washes over Frankie, bringing whispers. The whispers.

They spiral up out of the darkness, speaking the unintelligible gibberish of the other world. Murmurs from beyond the veil. Utters from the realm of the dead.

They drill with deafening muttering, with piercing hints, with stabbing sighs of loss. They grow louder, deeper. Maggots of memory lick into Frankie's brain as he collapses to his side, hands clamped over his ears, legs drawing up as he goes into a fetal curl.

He cries, cringing, trying to make himself smaller. Anything that might help to ease this penetrating agony.

Reaching a soul-chewing pitch, the whispers stop as abruptly as they began.

Total complete silence. A brooding quiet. An announcing pause. And then... from that black, webbed mouth come children's voices, high and clear.

And cruel.

Mean, singing voices filled with spite. Voices filled with taunting, twisting malice.

"Daddy loved us, this we know,
For the darkness tells us so.
Mommy, mommy never came near,
Never, ever held us dear.
Daddy, daddy held us tight,
Till the blood soaked him bright."

Above Frankie, the wraiths show themselves. There is no gradual materializing. There is nothing there... and then there is.

Like ropes of thick luminescent smoke, they weave around one another, forming a slow-turning circle. Each has a face. One at a time they dive toward him, almost touching, then pull back into their ghastly carousel.

Gaunt children's faces twist and stretch into ever-changing portraits of torment, hate, and want. Hints of color swirl as they dart, recoil, and dart again. Rotting teeth bare as they shriek.

They are children playing. Lost and horrific children from beyond. This is what they know. This is what they have felt. All they have ever known and felt.

Beneath this turning circle of hell, Frankie cowers. Tightly balled up and whimpering in the lonely attic dust. No one could fight this. His movie lore is just bullshit from old black and white films. This is torture, this is agony-dripping reality.

Knowing that there have never been any reports of a ghost ever hurting anyone, is worthless. It's as much crap as his movies. As empty as his life.

All three spirits snake their glowing twisted faces down within inches of him, still revolving, chanting through their crumbling teeth.

"Ready Rover! RL did come over,
And brought Wanky Frankie too!
But they chose the wrong door,
And didn't find Fatty Four-by-Four.

Shamey, shamey, RL's to blamey,
Whatever shall we do?
So we sendy send Gary,
To make the RL pay his due!"

And another draft of foul wind bursts from the black hole. Icy and clammy, wrapping around Frankie like the arms of a corpse. And the voices sing on.

"Bring us your mammy black,
And RL just might come back!

But he failed our gamey game,
So he won't be the samey same.

And Frankie Wanky, don't you run.
Not to tell mommy, she's no fun.

Or Mr. Bossy blue shirt,
will be more hurty hurt!"

And then, with snickering laughter fading behind them... they are gone. Leaving behind a shivering, bereft, terrified boy child.

Frankie slowly uncurls. He rises to his knees and stares into the funnel. All is quiet now. Dust motes drift through the flashlight's fading beam. Gary's skull still perches at the rim, abandoned and dead.

Abandoned like Frankie. Dead like RL.

"I... I'm sorry, RL," Frankie whispers. "I'm, I'm a coward. I can't come down there. I can't... I can't do anything."

Standing, he crosses to the spot where the skeleton had moldered for years. He picks up the Bible that he'd left. He stares at it, and begins to cry again.

All his lies about knowing haunted houses got RL killed. And delivered to this boy his first real heartache, his first true loss.

...I told him it would fall apart, I told him it was not real... I told him... He can't be gone... he can't be gone... he can't...

Squeezing the Bible with his good hand, as if to hurt the book. As if to milk from its dry pages a comfort he cannot reach.

Wiping his nose, Frankie walks back to the funnel's edge. He takes a deep, hitching breath, staring at the black hole.

He throws the Bible hard, it strikes the skull, and both tumble into the still darkness below.

"I'm so sorry, RL. And I'll... I'm... I will always love you."

He trudges back to the rusty iron trunk and sits, staring blankly at two unopened doors.

...I must tell Jayderay he's gone... I must be man enough to at least do that... But I can't... I just can't...

— ◆ ◆ ◆ —

Downstairs, as Shadow lunges to catch the falling Elvis, Jayderay tears free and bolts through the bedroom door, straight for the hidden stairs. Her heart is a beast. It has devoured all reason.

Behind her, Shadow scoops Elvis into her crooked arms, spins and rushes to stop the desperate woman.

Jayderay freezes with one foot on the first step, staring up into the dark, cold, forbidding passage.

Love is strong.

So is terror.

Both can kill.

Softly, she pleads, "Please, Lord... help me. I gotta go to him. I got to help. Please, help me. Please."

Behind her, carrying Elvis, Shadow reaches the hall and shouts, her voice shaking the walls:

"YOU WILL NEVER RETURN!"

⸻ ✦ ⸻

Sitting on the cold iron trunk in the colder attic room, Frankie breathes deeply, trying to be calm, trying to think.

...They said RL can still be hurt. Then maybe he's alive. If Nostra is too, then he's behind one of those doors. He's got to be! But if I choose wrong... I'll never get a chance at the other one...

His hand throbs; his heart hurts worse. Loss is a pain that nothing but time can ease. And Frankie has no time. Not for hurt, not for loss, not for crying. This lost little boy must become an adult, must do... something.

...And they said not to run to mommy... But wait! Shadow will already know... she will have felt it... That's not the same thing as me running to her. Is it? No! If she knows, then Jaderay knows... I won't have to break the news...

Frankie needs to stop both of the headstrong women. For certain, neither can be ordered, and herding women is dangerously impossible. He'd rather attempt charging at tanks. But the ghost taunts throb in his skull:

Bring us the black mammy.
Don't run to mommy.
RL can still feel hurt.

...No, it's more than I need to stop them, I have to stop them. If Shadow comes up here, or does anything, RL is gone forever. And Jayderay must not come, that would play right into those little bitches' hands...

———— ✦✦ ————

Shadow's shouted warning doesn't stop Jayderay. It was needless. Slowly, trembling, she turns away from the steps.

"It don't matter what you say, Shadow. I can't make myself go, God don't help, and I'm shamed. I'm too afraid—"

She is cut off by Frankie's stomping gallop down the steps.

He has heard Shadow's voice. Along with all the dead in China.

As Frankie steps to the floor, Jayderay throws her arms around him. Both break down, sobbing. Neither will say it, but they're both afraid RL is dead.

They babble over one another: apologies, questions, fear, love; a mother and son in ruin. But there is hope, overall, there is hope. There has to be.

Shadow watches silently.

For one brief moment, infinite sadness crosses her scarred face. A grief for love she never had—the love of and for children. That love had been stolen from her long ago by bestial cruelty.

As this unfolds, Elvis squirms in Shadow's arms like a toddler would. His lavender skin flushes to a ghastly purple. He's blushing.

"Shadow," he whispers desperately into her ear, "you can't carry me."

"Elv-is, there is no reason that I cannot—"

"I'm, I'm a man," he breaks in, pleading. "Baby... I'm, I'm embarrassed."

The male ego is fragile. Even ones from out of a test tube or petri dish.

Reluctantly, and very much against her better judgement, Shadow lowers her husband.

Frankie and Jayderay are still mother and son babbling, they are unaware that the he-man Elvis is being unleashed.

Elvis stands, knees on spindle legs quiver and knock together, but he will go. He must. He takes two heroic steps toward the pair.

And the determined hero promptly collapses, cracking his head on the wall, and bouncing it hard off the floor. He is completely out. Either knocked unconscious, or back into a coma, but he is gone.

Yes, Elvis is indeed a man. He has shown everyone.

Shadow cries out as he falls, diving with bent arms, trying but failing to catch him. She gathers him up for the second time, rising effortlessly, cradling her husband. And anger has taken her. She glares at Frankie; her grinding teeth audible.

"You did not even try to stop his fall! I, nor Elv-is, will leave the bedroom again," she hisses, her eyes beginning to change. A single tear trails down to ebony lips.

"I will not allow any chance of further injury to my husband. Frankie, you must find the witch-man you brought. He is now the only hope for RL."

"Then RL *is* alive?"

"In some manner they both are," snaps Shadow, her eyes beginning to all-white, scars darkening. "Yes. I sense their life, but I fear it may not be the same. Jayderay, you may come. Frankie, you may not. This... this fiasco is yours to deal with, you will not cower in my room."

Shadow whirls about, her gown swirling as gray as she, and carries her man, as his head lolls on her shoulder. She leaves no doubt; there will be no further help from her.

And also making one thing very clear: this is Frankie's mess to clear up. He brought the Medium. It is his burden. Life is indeed unfair; Frankie didn't cause this. But it's his now. Only his.

"Yes, Shadow," he murmurs fearfully.

"This all my fault, Frankie," Jayderay whispers. "If I hadn't run out of—"

A rumbling from the attic above interrupts her. Echoing down the steps, like foot falls of doom.

It's the sound of rupturing, splintering, exploding wood.

Shadow is right.

Those two men are not the same.

CHAPTER 17

WHILE BACK IN THE WAYDOWNS

Impatient with the dithering, imbecilic girl, who has evidently forgotten the way, Dr. Moto brushes past her. Looking back and giving her a withering look of disgust, he turns the corner without looking. Like an imbecile.

The Waydowns is quick to punish all stupidity, and medical degrees are absolutely no protection. Along with the slow, the weak, and the just plain fucked, the Waydowns solves all their problems.

The eaten have no problems.

Moto collides chest-first into something warm, slightly yielding, and very *wrong*. The impact bounces him staggering backward, dropping the chair leg. His heel slips, and he goes down hard, landing on his back with a sharp oofing sound. It's a sound that is rather... imbecilic.

Towering above them, something exhales. Hugely. It's a breath beyond foul; it's a breath that could peel paint.

Shrieking, the girl scrambles back, slamming into the corridor wall. The glass shard drops from her hand, skittering away on the deck.

Moto lies very still, dead still, and hoping the girl shuts up. Or that it gets her first. Perhaps by breathing on her.

Whatever he has ran into, shifts its weight, moving slightly. The haze parts in slow, lazy folds, and a shape appears, not fully, but enough to see that it's tall, it's way too close, and that it's... *considering*. As if weighing its options.

The air smells of sheared copper, wet meat, and old fat. In addition to that maggot gagging breath.

Moto keeps his eyes half-lidded, breathing shallowly through his mouth. He does not reach for the pistol. He does not move. He catalogues instead.

... Not a Coiler, or tentacles would've already yanked me up. Not an Eeed, it's too upright. Not a Spill, it's too small... it's much larger than any ape... unless some gorilla has been fucking a mattress...

This unknown makes some noises. Not speech exactly. Not quite. And definitely not comforting.

It's more of a thoughtful clicking, like joints being tested. Like lubricated connections. Like knotted muscles being readied. Like... not good.

Or maybe the bastard's stomach is growling.

The girl presses herself flat to the wall, eyes wide, white showing all around the pink. She makes a thin, keening sound in her throat and then clamps both hands over her mouth.

The thing leans down closer to Moto. Clumps of coarse dark hair grow indiscriminately all over its body. They look green. Dark green.

Through slitted eyes Moto continues to watch. He sees different parts of it. Too much of it. Any at all would be too much. This creature does not terrify him as the Gunch does... but he knows ripped-apart-death when he sees it.

Its skin hangs in folds, stitched and re-stitched, as though the creature has been assembled and repaired many times with whatever was available. Metal staples. Fiber cable. Old insulation. Something like teeth are embedded along its forearms. They're not in mouths; they're just teeth... growing there.

Parts for future reference, perhaps. Ease of brushing, maybe.

Dr. Moto knows that not all of the ship's lab discards are failures, not all are brain impaired Spills. No, sometimes a scientist who has gotten too big for his britches, or has a severe attack of swollen ethics, gets dumped down here.

And there's enough abandoned lab equipment around for one of them to set up shop. And practice a lot. Moto reasons he is probably looking at the results.

The thing's head tilts forward. Something drips from it onto Moto's chest. The spot begins to heat, and smoke rises. Its spit is acidic, and is slowly eating through the fabric of his coat. And soon will be eating through Moto.

But the Honorable Dr. Moto does not react. He keeps his honorable ass very, very still.

Letting his eyes flutter, and face slacken, he releases a small gasp. He's helpless, he's given up, he's fucking died. It's a good performance. Moto knows this... he's used it before.

The creature pauses, straightens, withdrawing slightly, and emits a low, clicking gurgle of a sound. It's disappointed.

From deeper back in the mists, another gurgle answers. And then another click. And then another gurgle... and so on.

It would seem this area of the Waydowns is crowded. And they too are disappointed. They had wanted a show. This is considerably less than comforting to Moto. These walking mattresses are intelligent.

The creature steps back, clearing space as some of its brethren shift behind it. More indistinct shapes move farther back. The fog drifts, thinning more, and reveals some *architecture.*

Not original ship, nor parts from the melding holo- caust. This is Do-it-Yourself habitation. Walls made of layered trash, broken furniture, ripped out lockers that have been tied together with pieces of chewed electri- cal cable. And there's a pathway entry, its edges worn smooth by repeated passage.

This is not a place these hulking monsters just stum- bled into by chance.

No. This is a village.

And the *dead* Moto, files this knowledge away. This may be of use at a later time, but right now it's only a place that he dares not run toward.

The creature clicks and gurgles again, then reaches down. And Moto nearly shits. But the reach was not for him, but for that glass shard the girl had dropped. Moto breathes again. And stills his bowels.

Lifting it delicately between two fingers, this cobbled together thing examines it, turning it so the light catches and sparkles along its edge. It seems fascinated.

Abruptly, it jabs the piece of glass toward the girl. It takes a step, clicking and gurgling with an entirely dif- ferent pitch. It sounds happy. It is. It's having fun.

The girl is not; she sobs silently, terrified. This is far from her home area, and she's never encountered any creatures like this before.

Running had been her first impulse, but... there's the kindly old man and her meat reward to consider. Plus, she's counting on the old man to pull his gun.

And hoping he isn't really dead.

Watching the creature move toward the girl through slitted eyes, Moto decides to produce the gun, even though he hasn't checked it since the misfire. He needs the girl.

But he does regret having to quit the corpse act; watching this stitched and quilted together thing is fascinating. Plus, it and the tribe seem to have put up some type of commune. Rather amazing that they wouldn't use a ship area. There is certainly no shortage of rooms. Why? These overstuffed fucks aren't just smart; someone is directing them.

But needs must. He has to act; the girl knows the way out. He must not lose her to a giant couch.

Moto silently pulls the pistol, points, and rises from the deck.

He's hoping with all of his shriveled soul that this hulking beast knows what a gun is. And will be fearful, because he suspects it would take all his bullets just to stop it.

And maybe not then.

The creature turns its head toward him. And that clicking gurgle stops. It knows, yes, it knows exactly what a gun is. This knowledge gives Moto considerable courage compared to the corpse he'd been imitating.

"You are quite a specimen," says Dr. Moto, calmy and bravely. Brushing at his still acid smoking front, he continues. "Yes, indeed, you're definitely the product of some diseased sphincter's fevered experimenting, aren't you? I've done much of the same in my time," he continues conversationally. "Though mine have generally had a more palatable appearance."

Silence.

"Nothing to say? Perhaps your creator did not teach you manners. It doesn't really matter, it's obvious you know what a pistol is. Correct?"

Silence.

"Oh, how rude of me, you don't wish to talk. Or you're just too stupid. Too bad, for I would very much like to find out how you *do* know what a firearm is. And who it is that manufactured you. Oh well, perhaps another time?"

Silence.

"You're a devilish hard fellow to have a conversation with, I must say. You're even worse than that idiot girl standing over there urinating on herself."

Silence.

And then it... *laughs*.

It is a truly horrible sound. The noise of air forced through cavities not meant for it. An intelligently cruel chuckle. But it is unmistakably amusement, this creature is not afraid.

The glass shard drops from its hand. It takes one step back, then another, and turning, retreats into the mists.

The others follow.

Moto notes that it did not run. It knew what a gun was, no doubt, but not overly frightened of it. He slowly nods to himself; the beasts are following orders. Or he and the girl would be dead, regardless of the pistol.

Silence reigns at the village, thick and listening.

Moto, still wipes at the corrosive spit-drip on his coat with distaste. Evidently, it's meant only for flesh, and fizzles out on other materials. Even in the Waydowns there can be rare good fortune.

He turns to the girl. Looking at her with even more distaste, he sighs.

"Well, my little quivering pile of misalignment, that encounter was certainly educational. I dare say even you have learned which way *not* to go. Yes, even such as you will have gotten that."

"Ba," she says softly still looking where the mattresses had disappeared. "Ba," she repeats.

"Yes, 'ba' indeed, my dear. How astute of you."

The pink eyes filming with tears, she speaks.

"Ank oo."

It's said simply, but with reverence. This is twice she thinks the Great Moto has saved her.

Dr. Moto would agree with this; he is great. Besides, he owns her, so the saving of his property deserves thanks.

"Yes, yes, I'm sure you're once again brimming with groveling gratitude, my dear. But we have no time for it. After having to deal with some demented shit's experiment, we are behind. So... on to More Topside!"

He smiles. Benignly.

Picking up the chair leg, he points it away from the village of the beasts.

"That may not be the route that you know," he says, jabbing with the leg, "but we now have no other choice. So, my dear, you will find another way. You will find... More Topside. Or there is the chair leg."

He smiles. Benignly.

She understands the "more topside" and the pointing is obvious; there is no other way. And the man's smile is reassuring as always.

A bit later, Moto does allow them a long enough break for him to check out that non-firing pistol. And finds everything looking just fine. Hmm. He thinks about firing a test round back at the village, but only briefly. There would be the noise, and might stir up that tribe of king size beds. Better to write the misfire off to a bad cartridge for now.

The pair walk on, further into this new corridor. Ahead, tired caution lights blink through the perpetual haze. Like far away dying stars. Caution indeed.

Behind them, the mists slowly drift over and through the village. From the shadows, several hulking forms silently appear. Each carry something.

And they follow.

CHAPTER 18

IN THE ATTIC

The sound of shattering wood from the attic explodes down those once secret steps.

Jayderay and Frankie jump into each other's skin, and locking hands, they run to Shadow's room. Only with her can anyone in this house be totally safe.

But they do not go inside just yet.

One of them is not currently welcome. And Frankie is not eager for any confrontation with that woman. He would prefer going back to the attic. Much prefer it. The charcoal toned woman is beyond frightening when angry.

"We shouldn't ought to have run, Frankie. What if... what if it was... could it maybe be RL? It might be him—"

"No," he breaks in, thinking of that awful webbed funnel in the attic floor. That crash they heard was not the Boss. They're not lucky enough for that; this is the Roaton house.

"If that was RL, he'd already be down here, or yelling for us."

"Then what was it? You been up there, Frankie! Could it be that fat Hoodoo man?"

Frankie lies. He's good at it. Almost as good as RL.

He's already told her that RL had vanished in billowing clouds of dust and dark as they were moving junk around. That he had been there one second, and then just gone. That spared her the horror of hearing about the web. Jayderay doesn't need that awful vision crawling through her thoughts.

"Well, me and RL left furniture and junk stacked and leaning around all over the place up there while we looked for Nostra. That noise was probably just a piece of it falling over we didn't stack right," says Frankie, figuring this sounds reasonable... and fearfully wonders what it really is.

And he's having a vision of *something* big making that crashing noise. As it tore its way out of a web funnel. Something with way, way too many legs, and a very bad attitude. Possibly carrying a mangled body.

"Frankie... what we gonna do?" she asks, her voice thick with tears. "I, I know what I should do, I'll, I'll force myself to go up those—"

"NO!" his word comes out nearly a scream.

"If you go, the wraiths will take you. Shadow said they would. And now that I've seen them, I know I can't fight them. No one could. And if they take you, then what happens to RL?"

"Then what, what we..." her voice breaks, and she falls against him.

Frankie holds her as she cries, and *he* wants to cry. Again. He wants to cry buckets until they overflow. And wash away their loss and fear; like tears are supposed to. But in this house, tears have no power.

No, Frankie can't cry again. There is to be no false refuge of tears for this man. This unlikeliest of saviors. This hero wearing a dirt and snot smeared chartreuse ensemble. He has no time; no time for weeping.

This trembling noble fool must climb back into the attic. He must find Nostra.

There will be no *look for*. There will be no *try*. And with bravery or luck, a ton of both, he will *find* Nostra. Frankie must find that Medium. But this house is known for twisting luck. Frankie needs to be careful of what he wishes for.

If RL lives, Nostra is his only hope. And if Nostra lives, he is also Jayderay's only hope. Everything depends on a fat man who wears a dress. All of which means Frankie... has gotten the shaft in this mess.

And there's no gold at the bottom of this shaft.

But probably a lot of legs.

—————— ✦ ——————

At the base of those once secret stairs, Frankie looks up into that silent, swallowing blackness. He stands alone. This is his to do.

With RL, Frankie has fought horrific mutations in the Waydowns. He had dodged, hacked, bled and screamed during a desperate rescue of Jayderay. He had emerged shaken... but still very much Frankie.

But this attic. This damned-to-another-world attic. This attic is a place of hell. A place of nightmare unending. Of constant emotional flagellation. Of soul pollution. If he lives through this... he will not be Frankie.

Frankie is without doubt, a silly, giggling, dangerous-joker of a man. A man whose sincerity is that of a one-night stand's promise. An ephemeral man. And he has no regrets about this. None. And he would not consider himself a loss to anyone.

But this man can love. Deeply. And love is why he stands here at this entry to hell.

He starts up the stairs.

Using another flashlight, he aims the beam at the steps, where it nearly dies on contact.

Frankie doesn't blame it; he feels the same way. Step by lonely, dirty step he continues. The walls lean in, cold seeps from them, his hand throbs.

He begins to hear something. It's not really a spooky something, but a human something.

A *living* human something, and one that's mumbling. It doesn't sound happy, but Frankie definitely is. A living person counts for a lot in this cursed place.

... It could be RL... but no, of course not... that would be too easy, and there is no easy around here. Well, it's alive, I'll hold on to that... it's all I've got... I just hate this fucking house...

The mumbling continues, and so does Frankie. As his eyes become level with the attic floor, he stops, holding the light steady.

...well, it sure as shit ain't RL...

... it's... Buddah.

"Nostra! Where in the God damn hell have you been?" demands Frankie, stepping up into the room.

Sitting hunched on the iron trunk, shoulders slumped, head hanging, Nostra ignores him. He looks as if he caught and battled the Bubonic Plague. And lost.

This is a broken Buddha. Broken by this attic. Broken by the house. Broken beyond repair.

He keeps mumbling, rocking slightly, hands dangling. Tears drip from his face onto the dust swirled floor. His star emblazoned dress is filthy, and dirt shows in the fat creases of those chins.

"Those poor... those poor... no, no, no," he murmurs. "Poor, innocent, defenseless... What monstrous evil... What bottomless cruelty. Oh, my God... Oh, my Lord... how could you allow... why?"

He continues mumbling, spiraling deeper into his grief. It's not a life changing grief. It's life ending.

Frankie looks on for a few seconds, keeping the light trained on this spectacle. This is no longer the showboat, fat Pansy he once knew.

"Nostra." Frankie speaks softly now. "What... what has happened? Where, uh, where have you been?"

Slowly the Medium turns his head. With a face the color of unclean snow, he looks spectral, diseased, badly used. He looks used up.

He fixes Frankie with hollow, hope forsaken eyes.

"Where have I been?" he responds, the voice hoarse.

"Why, I've been in this house is where I've been, Frankie. Oh, God damn fuck yes! In this house that you called me to. In this house that you forced me into. Oh, God damn fuck yes, I've been in this house."

He barks out a horrible, bitter laugh. "I've seen this house, Frankie. I've walked this house. I've walked ALL OF IT! I've walked it alone. I will walk it forever. Because of you...you shit. You simpering, lying little trickster. You never told me what was here. You unutterable, stinking shit."

"Yes, I guess I am," quietly responds Frankie, wondering if this shattered man is any longer sane. Or is dying. He watches this wreck of a Medium for a few seconds, feeling guilty.

"Look, I'm sorry," he continues. "I truly thought the house was just haunted, I really didn't know anything more than—"

"Just haunted? Just haunted!" hisses the Medium, spit spraying. "You ignorant, sad, sad, little queer. Fuck you!"

"I'm... I'm sorry, Nostra. Really, I am. Is there any way I... uh, I can help?" saying this, Frankie is sincere. He reaches his injured hand to the man's shoulder.

The Medium slaps it away, surging to his feet.

"Help? You want to help, do you?" he asks from a froth dripping mouth.

Storming to one of the closed doors, he grabs the knob.

"Then help!" he shrieks, jerking the door open.

Inside, rotted window curtains hang in shreds, allowing a dim wretched light into an anguish laden, terrible room.

Frankie stares, slowly sinking to his knees.

The flashlight falls from his lifeless fingers, rolling across the wooden floor. Its beam spraying out against desolate walls.

He vomits.

CHAPTER 19

A WAYDOWNS IDOL

Moto and the girl move deeper into this unfamiliar corridor. This white metal hallway, where bruised looking fog rolls above, and its floor stretches into forever.

Nothing down here is known anymore. Not really. Whatever maps or schematics once existed were lost decades ago. The melded decks of that botched experiment and the ensuing holocaust have made them all worthless. Hallways, corridors, rooms, all are unknown in this realm of the lost. Nothing down here is any longer recognizable. Not to anyone. Not to anything.

But being unmapped territory, doesn't keep the Waydowns from being a very busy place. It teems with life. Often heard, and more often... unseen.

The girl knew a few areas close to her home, but not here. The beast village had blocked that way, forcing them into this territory she has absolutely no familiarity with. None. But she will try for the kind old man. She's sure he must miss his home as much as she does hers.

She moves cautiously now, picking her way through the endless trail of trash, destruction, mutiny, and abandonment. At each open hatch, she pauses, peering inside, taking a few tentative steps in, checking. Something may lurk inside, and might follow after them through the haze. It would not be for fellowship. She keeps her glass shard ready; whatever might be hiding will not announce itself.

Surprises in the Waydowns are usually the last surprise anyone gets. A strict one-to-a-customer policy. One is enough.

Dr. Moto is not yet too impatient. He does understand the necessity of going slow. But this uncharacteristic patience will not last. Moto isn't being nice; he's just being careful. And holding back the chair leg... for now.

The girl is trying hard at this hopeless task of finding a new route to the Topside door. She wants desperately to please the kindly old man, but she is a long way from her home area. And there is absolutely nothing familiar. Only more halls, openings, and the endless white metal corridor, always looking the same. And passing open hatches with their long-abandoned work stations and still blinking lights. Still waiting for staff that will never come back. Only death returns to this place.

Continuing on slowly, the girl trying to find something recognizable as a guide post. Something, anything.

Being lost makes missing her own home more intense. It has water from the wall and she can sleep safe. Her Da had found it.

Moto flashes her that oriental smiley face regularly, and nods encouragement. He has plenty of both, and they cost him as much as they mean. But he is infinitely sick of her.

Pacing the girl, he constantly keeps a wary eye out for anything moving. He thinks of the Eeed's length and girth, and feels it will not be satisfied with just part of a Spill's leg. But an elderly scientist and dirty girl would be just right.

Thinking of this, he slowly pats the chair leg in his palm. Lovingly. It could provide great inducement for the girl to hunt harder and move faster. Not to mention providing considerable entertainment for Moto.

Dr. Moto keeps one eye on the roiling vapors high above, but no longer ignores the corridor itself. Meeting the Eeed and beast had taught him that lesson. Survival here demands attention in all directions.

And a startled grunt from the girl makes him very attentive. He steps quickly to the hatch she's investigating.

She flashes him a crooked, embarrassed grin and points upward with the shard.

At the junction of ceiling and wall, a support strut once offered refuge. Some poor bastard climbed up there during the holocaust and held on.

He's still holding on.

And he's disturbingly intact. A lab coat clings to his shriveled frame; his arms locked in a death-grip around the strut. His torso is wedged against the ceiling. And his shrunken eyes glare down, frozen in accusation.

It's not hard to determine the cause of death. Below the groin, there is nothing. That'll do it, every time.

Shreds of trousers dangle, and blood stains mark where the rest of him had been. And had been slowly taken.

Whatever plague infected staff member, or fast mutating lab animal had killed him, they had worked hard at it. Leaping high, again and again, tearing off a piece each time. The man must have kicked frantically, trying to dodge ripping teeth as he pushed himself higher.

At least he had while his legs were still attached.

The scene interests Moto in a detached, clinical way. He studies the remains, wondering how long the man lasted before bleeding out. Judging by his still locked-on grip of that strut, quite some time.

Moto nods, approvingly. The labbie had been of exceptional stock. He wishes the turd had been one of his test subjects. Moto's experiment animals of all kinds had tended to give up early. And eagerly.

"Ba!" the girl exclaims sharply.

Moto turns to her at once. The girl doesn't use that word over a hangnail.

Midway up the wall, a slowly pulsing patch of Gunch clings to the metal, and it's about the size of a large skillet. Shiny puke yellow. Several arm-like protrusions have grown from it, reaching out. Searching for food victims, and turning the mass into something like a flattened octopus. It bubbles and softly pops as it breathes, each tiny rupture spreading microscopic wet fragments farther outward.

Sending out babies.

Few things terrify Dr. Moto. He has created too much horror himself to be truly terrified of anything. Except for this yellow shit, this Gunch... it fucking well does. The thought of dissolving slowly for years, being absorbed and knowing it, is a horror beyond all others.

He shudders visibly and backs away toward the corridor, all bravery gone.

"Yes, yes, it is *Ba*," he snaps, waving the girl back frantically. "Now move, you bleating idiot, before it gets on you! It'll make you part of the organism."

...I could not bear watching that, even on her... And I still need this odiferous sheep.

His warning isn't needed, but she is touched by the concern it shows. Truly touched. She increases her resolve to help him, to find another route to Topside. She owes this kind old man.

Behind them, deeper in the fog that cloaks the beast village, shadows stir.

Shambling forms shift, quilted and stapled skins pull tight, and teeth ache as they grow wrongly. These creatures endure pain silently. They've been taught this. Better to endure... than be tossed into the Master's vat.

And they have a task. These beasts have orders, and each carry something that will be needed. Moto and the girl are being tracked.

Back in the huge white hallway, Moto watches the girl navigate. His patience thins.

... here I am, the Honorable Dr. Moto, being led by this non-witted subhuman. Being kept from exacting my very just revenge on those two round-eyes and their delectable Negress. Those who have the stolen breastplate-portal, those who crept through it into the ship, those who kidnapped my honorable ass, those who took me to their Roaton house, those who forced me to medicate that ridiculous Elvis creature... those who...

An airborne screech cuts through this mental rant, and Moto freezes. He well knows, the Waydowns punishes wool-gathering. The gatherer is likely to get gathered.

Both he and the girl look back down the echoing corridor, peering through the drifting haze. She clutching her glass shard, he with raised chair leg, and one hand on the gun.

Far behind them, they dimly see tentacles that have dropped from the murky heights. And see two wrapped shapes thrash and vanish upward into the mists, dropping their primitive choke-poles. Gargling, clicking screams echo and then stop. There are no follow up sounds.

The village beasts had not known what Coilers were.

Or where they lived.

They do now.

The mission for their Master has ended for these two. Rather unsuccessfully. But their creator did send others. Smarter specimens that are better equipped, and will not need to look up.

Not knowing what has happened, other than a Coiler banquette, Moto urges the girl forward. Whatever is happening behind them does not require spectators. But he does increase his own upward looking.

They still move at a slug's pace, and the girl is near tears, lost and desperate to please. All the while, Moto fights the urge to introduce the chair leg as motivation. He promises himself this treat will come soon.

Taking another quick look up at the drifting, often turbulent fog high above, he wonders if any Coilers might at this very moment be eyeing him. Thinking of inviting a Moto up for tea. Reportedly, they have a lot of eyes.

Looking over at the girl, he snorts in disgust. It's obvious she is still lost, and hasn't the slightest clue of which way to go. Squinting through the haze, shaking her head, scratching herself in various places. And then doing it all again. Especially the scratching.

... Oh, yes, scratch, by all means, scratch. Perhaps that will stir up something besides your fleas, you worthless amoeba brained drudge. I almost wish a Coiler would drop a couple of tentacles down. I'd get the joy of hearing you scream "Lers, Lers" as they yanked you up for dinner... and your putrid smell would ascend as well...

Then, through thinning haze, they see... something that isn't *right*. Nothing is ever right in the Waydowns, but this is something that absolutely should not be here.

Something tall. Huge. And very *still*. Nothing in these twisted corridors remains upright, everything has been knocked down, plundered, ruined. Or it's alive and moving.

Or it's dead. If dead, then lots of smaller things like Spills should be moving about it, feeding. But nothing stirs around this thing.

Ahead, the massive shape squats in the center of the passage. The girl knows something is badly wrong about this. She's hasn't survived down here without being able to know danger when she sees it. She stops.

"Ba," she warns quietly.

"Oh, do be quiet," responds Moto in a casual tone. "It isn't alive, you little colostomy bag." He is intensely curious, but not worried. This is part of the original ship; anything this huge has to be.

The girl remains standing still, nervously clutching her glass knife. Knowing that it could hardly be effective against anything this big, but it's all she has.

Moto moves closer, leaving the girl behind. He squints, studying the thing with a puzzled expression. He feels that what he's seeing should not be possible. Not here.

He steps closer. And closer.

... It's a... a... a fucking boulder? What type of Way-downs conjuring crap is this? There are no rocks down here... nowhere in the ship... no stone anything...

Moto steps even closer. There is no fear, only prudent caution, and that's fading rapidly into a scientist's intense curiosity.

...Yet, it is rock... Sandstone? ... Granite?...

It's not merely big — it's truly monumental. A towering stone cliff, much taller and wider than Moto. Obviously placed there, like some huge Pagan idol to be bowed down to and worshipped.

Cracks and crevices mar the otherwise smooth surface, indicating age... or rough handling when moved here.

Moto keeps puzzling over this thing, feeling that it's not dangerous, but not something to be ignored. It might even be helpful, possibly intended as a direction indicator, or a boundary mark.

... could it be some type of a guide or sign?... but where did it come from? What down here would need such a thing?... And why make it so huge?... I'll force the girl to climb it; she's half an ape and will be able to scale this...

Moto is truly stumped. He is now close enough to touch it, but does not. Dark stains spot the surface, and leaning in closer he detects the hint of a foul odor. Very foul.

... something has been crawling about on this, leaving scent... yes, I can see how a pervasive stink would attract scavengers hoping to find food... the odor is worse than the wretched girl...

Carefully walking around it, Moto finds the thing fairly smooth and featureless on all sides. Except for the occasional crack, there are no markings, no chiseled or painted arrow with words reading: Topside that way. Just rock, and the smell. Touching it for the first time, rubbing his fingers across it, he feels no particular difference in temperature.

... the texture is somewhat unusual... it is definitely some type of rock or stone... Yes, I must send the cave girl up this thing... it could be hollow...

With that thought, he raps the chair leg against it, and gets a sound as solid as... a rock. Nodding, he places a shoulder to it, pushing, and finds it as immovable as he thought it would be.

The girl has remained rooted to the spot behind Dr. Moto, and does not help with the pushing. She's worried by his examinations of this thing, wishing she had the words to tell him: "Don't fuck with that you idiot." She has no idea of what a rock or a stone is, much less a boulder, but she does know, this simply should not be here. It is wrong.

"All right, my dear, it is time for you to exhibit some of your innate simian abilities," says the smiling, kindly Dr. Moto. Pointing at her, he continues, "I want you to scamper, scamper mind you, up this." He emphasizes by tapping the rock with the chair leg, and pointing up.

"Ba," she says, shaking her head.

"No, no my dear," says the doctor with a smile, "It isn't ba, but this chair leg could defi—"

The stone moves.

Just a few inches.

Toward Moto.

His eyes pop as he jumps back. Glaring at it with more disbelief than fear.

No, not alive... it can't be... it's rock... it can't—

One of the cracks splits open with a squalling hinge sound. A mouth! And a stench of rotten life pours out.

Moto screams, turning to run.

The girl screams, already running.

Moto isn't fast enough. Slow is not rewarded in the Waydowns.

Shooting forward, this thing that can't be alive, this thing that has to be stone... spews out a nasty, greasy liquid, drenching Moto.

And gulps him to the waist. Outside that awful maw, his legs kick and churn furiously.

Dr. Moto is very old; he has earned and deserved death many times.

But eaten alive... by a carnivorous rock?

What a way to go.

CHAPTER **20**

WITHIN THAT ATTIC ROOM

As Frankie vomits, the Medium stands at the door looking on, breathing heavily. There is no sympathy.

This is no longer the corpulent shaman Nostra. No longer the fat Medium who arrived driving a star festooned hearse and wearing a turban.

That person is dead. This is a man who has crawled through filthy ditches of endless torment. A man who is less than he was... and much more. So much more.

"Do you still want to help, you little mincing faggot?" asks Nostra, gesturing through the open door.

Still on his knees, eyes locked on what's in the room, Frankie nods. Wiping his mouth, he slowly rises, speaking hoarsely.

"I will do whatever you ask."

Nostra silently walks into the room. Dirty sunlight leaks through tattered remnants of curtains. It shines dimly on horror. Old horror, forever fresh. Life staining horror.

Three wooden chairs, placed side by side, hold agony from long ago. Agony that's still there. And dust coats them as sagging cobwebs drape all together.

While facing the chairs, he speaks tonelessly to Frankie.

"Bring me my Bible. I must have it now." It is not a request.

Without a word, Frankie turns, walking toward the room of the funnel. The room of the skeleton. The room of the web. The room where he had thrown the Bible into depths unknown.

The room of whispers. The room of wraiths.

Speaking aloud, but softly to himself, he says, "I will crawl into that hole. I will bring back his Bible. No matter what, I will bring him that Bible. I must help. I will help."

At the door, he takes a deep breath and reaches for the knob. Before his fingers touch it, the door swings open.

RL stands there blinking, obviously unsure of where he is. Looking at Frankie with blank eyes, he says, "I, I think… I think… I was told you need this," holding out the Bible.

After what Frankie has just been shown by Nostra, the reappearance of RL is nothing. He gives him a disgusted, cursory up and down look.

"You're not even hurt. Did you find Alice and fuck her while you were down there?"

RL simply blinks at him, not speaking, confused beyond words.

Rudely jerking the Bible out of his hand, Frankie looks at him with undisguised loathing.

"Come on… *rabbit*, you need to be there, you need to see this," he says coldly.

RL follows without asking questions. The door closes softly behind him.

Reaching the room, Frankie immediately walks through, his face steeling itself.

RL stops motionless. A few seconds pass.

He whips his head away from the sight with a force that cracks his face into the doorjamb. He grips the wood with both hands as blood runs from his nose, dripping down, brightly red.

He speaks with a shredded voice, as from a throat full of glass.

"I will kill someone for this."

"No," replies Frankie. "There is no one, there's nobody to kill. All you can do is hurt. Like I do. And help us."

RL remains where he is, silently refusing. His face and hands still against the doorjamb, eyes resolutely looking away. Away into darkness. And still seeing three girls. He will never be free of the sight. They have become cankers in his mind.

Frankie steps to him, taking hold of an arm.

"I am in this hell because of you, RL. I brought Nostra here because of you. You *will* help. You will help us to help them."

RL nods with a jerking motion, smearing his blood on the doorjamb. Gritting his teeth, he allows Frankie to turn him to face into the room. This is a man who never knew compassion as a child. Ever. Because of that, he has a bottomless well of it for animals and children. For those who cannot speak for themselves. For those who have no one.

RL will help. He cannot do otherwise. That is not possible.

Nostra holds the Bible clutched to his chest. He looks at the three chairs.

There are children tied to them. Small children.

The cold attic has preserved them well.

Their feet are tied to the chair legs with rags. Rags from dresses that had been ripped off these little girls.

Nostra goes to each child. He strokes the dry, crumbling hair, he gently pats parchment skin and warped faces. He cries quietly.

And he kisses their arms, as flecks of dried skin stick to his lips. Skin from arms that are twisted behind each child. Arms that were repeatedly broken until they could be tied in a knot. Then, the children had waited. Waited for what came next.

"Yes, yes, child," he tells each one. "Poor, innocent, guileless child, you will be at peace. You will go to rest now. You will all go together. I will take you."

Finishing, he turns to the two watching men. He does not speak, but points to the floor. And he kneels before the girls.

Without a word, RL and Frankie kneel where they stand.

The Medium lowers his forehead to the Bible.

He does not speak. It is a short silence, but not a quick one. The difference can be profound. And very long.

Abruptly, he rises and faces the men. They slowly stand.

"The obese fool you called here has done his job. The children have gone. They are now at peace. I will never be."

He looks at them a few seconds longer, and then adds:

"You will inter the husks properly. You will be guided; you will know what is right."

Brushing past them without another sound, Nostra carries the Bible in one hand. The book pressed against his chest, beneath eyes that no longer see this world. He starts down those hidden steps he had never climbed.

He will not be seen again.

Not ever.

But he walks this house.

He walks it alone.

CHAPTER 21

AND IN THE WAYDOWNS

The girl screams as the boulder gulps Moto down to his waist. Clutching her useless glass knife, she backs away, gagging at the smell.

She watches as the old man's legs churn and thrash furiously. He still lives, but obviously it can't be for long. The smell alone will kill him.

The girl cannot make herself abandon the old man. Not like this. She must try to help. She must. He had shared his food. He had saved her. He always smiles kindly.

Holding her breath, she dashes forward, stabbing at the huge rock face. For all the good she does, she might as well be stabbing the ship's deck.

Retreating, she gasps for breath, expecting the monster to finish the job. To suck the rest of Moto in at any second.

The rock hasn't started chewing yet, perhaps savoring the Moto flavor first, before getting all of him in...

and then it will get serious. Or maybe rocks don't have or need teeth, and just swallow their dinner whole.

Taking another deep breath, she drops the glass shard, runs in, grabs the kindly old man by one leg, yanking with all she has. She's rewarded by the other leg delivering a kick to her face.

She backpedals to breathable air. The stench is beyond endurance.

Inside that cavernous maw, Dr. Moto is very much alive. He's passed the initial panic stage, and is starting to think. Frantic thinking, but coherent. And trying not to breathe. Breathing is not good. Breathing is foul, as foul as being inside a dinosaur's butt. A really big dinosaur. A dead one.

Except that he's not inside any kind of living creature. As soon as he had been gulped, he'd seen two village beasts, strapped by their waists to the upper walls, pulling at levers and turning wheels. A half empty vat of horrendous smelling lubricant at their shaggy feet. Enough to grease the rest of the Moto for that final gulp.

Though clamped tightly, Moto's torso and arms are free. He's cramped, but has enough room for some tight maneuvering.

And Moto has remembered, he still has the gun tucked in his waistband. Maybe he can squirm about enough get a hand on it, fire it. Maybe hell, he must. Even if he shoots his wiener off in the process.

Seeing that this awful creature has not yet slurped Moto in all the way, the girl takes a deep breath. And again, dashes to those still spasming, churning, bicycling legs.

Grabbing both ankles under her arm pits, she yanks.

Inside, Moto gets hold of the gun.

The girl pulls with all her might. And hears muffled pops from within the boulder. Her immediate thought was the thing had started chewing, and that the old man's legs might suddenly come free in her arms... without the old man.

More of those cracking sounds from within, and she's sure it's the crushing of his ribs. She sobs, and has to breathe. The stench is overwhelming her.

Knowing she won't be able to withstand much more of this putrid air, she puts her all into one last mighty pull.

And with the sound of a wet slimy cork, out pops the Honorable Dr. Moto.

An exceedingly wretched Moto. An exceedingly filthy Moto. An exceedingly unhappy Moto.

Trying to get her breath, the girl backs away. And then further back. And again. There is no escape from the intense, overpowering stink.

On his hands and knees, the good doctor retches. He retches quite thoroughly. He pauses, head hanging, possibly thinking about the quality of life. And then has another really good go at retching. He's becoming quite an expert at it.

Now, on his inside, Moto is exceptionally clean. Remarkably so. He has cleansed himself to the point of puking up his toes.

But on the outside, Moto... is not clean. From the waist up, he's smeared with a goo. A goo that Moto hopes, wants desperately to think, is nothing more than a lubricating jell. And not village beast feces. Hope springs eternal.

Regardless of intensely poor hygiene, his mind is still working. He grabs the gun he'd been shooting manically when he'd been squirted out. Pointing it at this Trojan Rock, fearing another engulfing might be imminent. It would be unlikely, since he had riddled the beasts with bullets. And when the girl had yanked him free, they had been hanging from their straps. Dead as... as rocks.

The boulder remains standing, towering there, looking unchanged, yet somehow dead. A dead trick-boulder. A dead ersatz-rock. The smell is appropriate for a dead anything that's huge. Even a T-Rex could be proud.

Understandably, Moto does not trust this rock. Nor will he ever trust another rock. Especially a big one. No, the good Doctor has learned: rocks are not trustworthy.

The Honorable Dr. Moto feels he's been an emetic. And he smells like a very used suppository.

Not trusting the mechanical rock, not trusting it even in death, Moto backs away to join the girl. Or tries to join her, but she keeps edging away from him... holding her nose.

Ripping his shirt off, he scrubs his face with the inside of it, wipes his hair and slings it away in disgust. This doesn't help.

The girl reaches out with a very stretched arm, offering him the last of the water. Which he snatches from her without a word, and uses every drop. There is a lot of spitting involved.

Looking at the girl, this mosquito hasn't a smile left to give. The odor had been too much for the insect; it's dead. There is no thank you either. He still grips the gun, and motions with it.

"More Topside," he croaks. He has a bad, lingering taste in his throat. Very bad, very lingering.

So, on they go, continuing down the bleak, trash filled corridor. And it's more of the same. The drifting haze, the occasional shriek echoing in the distance, the scuttling sounds of things unseen, and the constant danger. Moto spits regularly.

Behind them, the fog and mist creep over that treacherous, sneaky, swine of a rock. Inside it, the beasts hang, bleeding and dead. They will not be a burdensome loss to the village; there are plenty more.

But the boulder trap would indeed be a grievous loss. The Master will send others to dismantle and fetch it back. She had spent much time in its manufacture, with special attention to the lubricant-bait. It takes a lot of trapping to feed a village.

And she will be disappointed in this failure to catch the good Dr. Moto. She knows him from years past; from Deck 19. The memories are not fond ones. This vaguely human female has plans for him. And has no intention of giving up.

As Moto and the girl walk, one closed hatch is a bit different. A painted message on it, in sloppy, faded red letters, reads: PLAGUE HERE. Obviously some desperate labbie's attempt to keep the changelings out. And not be had for lunch.

Unable to read, but noticing its oddness, the girl points. And Moto responds with a surly shake of his smelly head.

"No, you little fool, there is no need to check. All that's in there will be a few starved to death idiots. 'Plague Here' indeed."

And Moto spits, as there's a terrible taste in his mouth. Absolutely horrid.

Sensing his mood, the girl remains in the lead, with the exceedingly fragrant Dr. Moto following. He notes that she seems quite willing to stay ahead of him. Almost eager.

Having just battled and defeated a monster, and a boulder of one at that, each of them hope for a brief lull. Just a small break from any attacks or other surprises.

Fat fucking chance, not in this place. The old adage, 'it never rains, but it pours' is true. And never more so than in the Waydowns.

Suddenly the girl squeals, jumping up and down, her coat flapping.

"Op Sigh! Op Sigh! she cries delightedly, jabbing the glass shard toward the distant mists.

Moto squints into the haze. Craning his neck forward as if that could possibly make him see better. Yes! In the distance... it is the topside door. The right one this time, and he's certain of it. Salvation is at hand, and even that taste in his mouth recedes.

It's an elevator door. It goes neither up nor down, it only slides open. Opening into the Roaton basement, into that cursed house. Where the Honorable Dr. Moto has much work to do. Extremely pleasurable work.

Moto is one huge smile. No mosquito required. He nods and nods, and smiles and smiles.

"You did it my little lump faced monstrosity! Indeed, you did. And I truly thank you, I do. And my thanks won't be all you'll be getting," says the kindly old man, gripping the chair leg.

The girl sees the smiles, understands the thank you, and grins her crooked mouth in return.

Moto wonders if he should club her now, just finish the girl and be done with the dirty, ugly thing. Or wait until they actually get to the door. Perhaps waiting would be best. He might still need her. But once the door is open, then he will have his payback for putting up her.

... yes, seeing that door slide shut with me in the Roaton house and her still in these wretched Waydowns... And what a lovely trip back to her hovel she will have, IF she can find her way. And the poor little dear is out of water...

"Come my precious dear," he says, motioning toward the distant door. Your luck will hold until we reach the door. He rewards her with more smiles. These are real, quite genuine smiles. Toothy.

And they continue on, the distance is not too far. Viewable even through the perpetual fog, the door is there. Soon, the good doctor will be in torturing heaven, and the round-eyes will pay. He's decided he will do the Negress first, while the other two are forced to watch. What delight! What euphoria!

But this is the Waydowns. It never rains, but it... shits.

Out of the mist and drifting fog, a scuttling, slithering sound echoes from the corridor. A noise of chitin against metal, the dragging of a huge carapace across the deck. And in seconds, that friendly Eeed appears.

Moto had been right; the Spill leg had not been enough to fill up the ravenous bastard.

It raises the large round face, turning it back and forth as it becomes visible through the haze. More of the body segments raise, lifting the head higher. The legs waving in the air. And on it comes. The head fixes on Moto and the girl.

Moto still holds the gun, and the girl edges toward him. Her glass knife is nearly useless against such a creature. The kind old man had saved her before, and she's sure he will again. This time the gun will fire.

On it comes, mandibles extend, withdraw, and extend, poison dripping, the upper legs waving. The entire front half of its body is now off the deck; the face is man high.

As before, Moto places his arm protectively around her shoulders, gun held in readiness.

On it comes, closer, closer, almost to the outstretched gun.

The girl whimpers.

Moto takes careful aim... and throws her into it.

As she screams, he runs, flying down the corridor, all caution gone. He sees the door; it is so close. That is what matters, that entrance. At last, the right fucking door. That is all that matters.

Behind him, the Eeed wraps its upper legs around the girl as she shrieks. The poisonous mandibles extend, and she keeps on screaming, stabbing with the glass shard.

Moto leaps over crap, kicks through stuff, dodges around... and he grins. There is no smile, this is a grin instead. A very real, very malicious grin of delight. And he runs full out, caution be damned.

The girl thrusts and slashes at the black face, feeling the red legs closing around her. She makes a desperate lunge, trying to wrench away. One of its pinchers spear through the lapel of the coat, pulling her back. She shucks it over her head, fighting the cloth, pushing it into that hideous face.

And the Honorable Dr. Moto runs on. Sweat streams and his eyes shine, fixed on the door, the door, there is the door.

The girl's coat rips, she jerks free, staggering backwards, falling, scrambling up, running, her breath coming in desperate gasps.

And Moto gallops, grinning and pumping his legs as hard as he can.

He runs until he has to stop himself quickly. Stopping so fast, he trips over his own feet. Falling, skinning elbows, knees and hands. Trash sticks to his bare arms, back and belly, as he raises himself up.

Looking incredulously, fearfully at the door. He's no longer grinning. Moto wants to cry.

Yes, Moto, this is the Waydowns. It never rains, but it shits.

After breaking free from those clutching legs, and falling, the girl is disorientated. Totally lost, crazed with fear, she sees an open hatch. Reaching it, grabbing the door, struggling, using all her strength to pull it closed.

Behind her, the Eeed fights and rips at the coat, pinchers snapping, black legs flailing against the cloth.

The girl battles with the hatch, its hinges stiff with nonuse, she strains and tendons pop, moving it a few inches with each jerk.

Freeing itself from the coat, the Eeed sways, turning its head back and forth, the legs wave, curling open, then closing. Chittering in an undulating high pitch.

And then it halts all motion except the head, which jerks, swiveling side to side in decreasing arcs. It freezes, locking in on the girl as she sobs, grunts, and hysterically pulls at the hatch.

Lowering its body to the deck, the Eeed moves with shocking speed. It isn't just coming; it's nearly on top of her.

Screeching in frustration, the girl gives up on the door, dives into the room, and frantically searches for a hiding place.

The creature stops at the threshold, raises its head a foot into the air. The face turns back and forth repeatedly. It lifts itself higher. Higher. Trying to zero in on the girl, trying to locate flesh.

Unable to pinpoint the girl, it drops back to the deck and slithers into the room after her. Uncountable legs make a dry rustling noise as the body segments ripple and glint blackly. It's very good at hunting meat. That is all it does. It will find her.

While back down the corridor, Moto still looks at the Roaton house entrance. That door. Staring at it in disbelief. Staring with terror, with horror, and with burgeoning madness.

Growing down one side of the door is a strip of bright yellow abomination of life. Wetly bubbling. Pods of different lengths growing out from the main body, some onto the door itself.

It has not yet spread to the control panel. But it's close. Very close, and it's the controls that Moto needs.

The Gunch is somewhat sentient. A strain of Leprosy from the stars. It retains things from those it absorbs, so this blot of nightmare knows what an exit is. And purposely grew itself along the door's edge. It wants out into the world beyond.

Without thought, Moto drops the gun, not even hearing its thump on the deck. He can no longer smell his own stench. Or taste the filth in his mouth. He is unaware of the trash sticking to his bare chest and arms, or of his scraped and bruised body.

This is his only way out. He cannot go back. The girl is gone. He cannot go anywhere else. Death is in all directions.

Fighting down panic, he takes a step closer. Glaring at this yellow, this Gunch, this barrier to his freedom. Sweat drenches him as he swallows repeatedly, convulsively.

Moto stands motionless, summoning courage. Many long minutes pass as he goes into a near trance. Knowing he has no choice. He must get very close to the control panel; it is busted from a long-ago spray of bullets. Studying it, he knows without doubt he can bypass the damage. But it is inches away from that glistening, bubbling horror.

He continues to stand, stare and think. Getting that close to this abomination of life will be an act beyond bravery. More time passes.

... I can do this... I HAVE TO DO THIS... I must not touch, but I can do this... I only need to pry the panel loose... I can do this... I must not touch, but I can—

He's violently shoved face first in the yellow wet growth. His scream is cut off by the glistening pod that slips into his mouth. Another follows, sealing over his lips.

Thrashing, wrenching, bucking, Moto cannot free himself. The Gunch has attached itself the full length of his body; once touched is forever.

All his fighting only manages to get his head turned to one side. And while he still has one eye not yet covered, he sees his attacker.

The crooked faced girl stands there watching.

"Ba," she says quietly.

With the few seconds of sight Moto has left, he watches her pick up his gun, and walk back down the corridor.

And then he is blind.

It takes quite a while for Dr. Moto to be totally covered. He fights and struggles, surging against the advancing translucent skin.

But pod by pod, tendril by tendril, the Leprosy cloaks him. But he doesn't die.

Moto will live for years. For many more long years.

He will be aware of it.

He will be aware of every second.

CHAPTER 22

HARD AND BLEAK

RL and Frankie decide to bury the girls behind the house. It seemed a fitting place, and it felt right. They asked for no one's approval or help. Even had they wanted, contact with a funeral home for coffins was out of the question.

This is theirs to do. And neither man would've had it any other way. They would not have allowed anyone else. The girls were their responsibility now.

It's decided that one grave for all three seems proper. They have been together for such a long time.

The bodies required some breaking to remove them from the chairs. Frankie ran a few steps aside and was quietly sick. RL simply cried, his breath hitching in his chest as he worked.

The tiniest of things can be heartbreaking; one small clenched fist held a stick of chalk. Another held a barrette. Another a nickel. What awful, meager items of comfort for a child to cling to. What a terrible, forsaken, bleak existence. How badly these two men wanted to kill the father.

But the pleasure of murdering the father was denied them. Long ago, that monster had chained himself to a stake. And his end had been much more agonizing that anything even RL and Frankie would have devised.

There was not a lot of digging required. With an old hand stitched quilt from the house as their shroud, the children make a pitifully small bundle. It hurts both men to see its size; there are three little children laying there. Little girls.

Considering Frankie's injured hand, RL offers to do the digging. Frankie shakes his head, saying, "I will manage." And he does.

They shovel for a while in silence. Then RL stops, jambs his spade into the dirt, and quits. He looks at Frankie with pent up exasperation.

"Okay, damn it, enough! What is it, what's wrong? You haven't said ten words to me. Not since you found me. And not much more to... even to Jayderay."

Frankie looks steadily at him for a time.

"You bastard, you weren't even hurt. And I didn't find you. You just popped out like a rabbit with that Bible in your hand, and no explanation. Had you been hiding... hiding and laughing at me?"

"No! Frankie, I've already told you... I don't know what happened; I don't remember shit. It's all a blank.

Would it have been better if I'd shown up, chewed to a pulp, and carrying my ass in one hand instead of the Bible?

"Yes. It would have." he says softly, looking directly at RL. "It... it tore my guts out when you fell."

"Look, I'm... I'm truly sorry. Really. I didn't exactly do it on purpose."

"Just forget it," says Frankie, in a curt, flat tone. And he goes back to his one-armed digging.

"Fine," responds RL, heaving a long sigh. And he goes back to his shovel.

After a short while, the children are placed in the grave, both men stand quietly, looking down at the sad and small roll.

"Shadow can't come outside," RL says, needlessly, adding "but I guess I should at least go tell her and Jayderay."

Frankie doesn't speak, continuing to look down.

Shaking his head, RL goes inside.

Hearing his steps, Jayderay meets him at the bedroom door, holding a finger to her lips.

Turning, she points at the bed where Elvis is asleep, with the gray woman hovering about him. Touching, stroking, gently kissing.

Possibly no man in history has ever been looked after better. Or any lavender mutant either.

But Elvis looks bad. Faded and fading. It's obvious that Shadow cannot see this. Or refuses to see, is more likely. The blinders of fear have snapped into place. Her man is good and getting better. Woe be unto any who would tell her otherwise.

As they all three step into the hall, Shadow stays at the door, her hand resting on the knob. She will not stray far or long from him.

"RL," Shadow begins without preamble. "I thank you for what you've done. For Jayderay and for my Elv-is. Those wrai— my daughters are well and truly gone. I feel it within me, within the fabric of the house."

"You are more than welcome, Shadow. Much more. I came to... I'm here to... uh, to ask if, uh, I mean what would you like for... should I—"

Interrupting him, Jayderay takes mercy on her fumbling man.

"RL, just hush. We both know why you here, ain't no... there is no reason for you to be embarrassed. Sakes, we all know she can't step outside."

"I feel no shame of this, RL," Shadow says gently with a small smile. "Those... my daughters, were denied contact with me. And I had no wherewithal to correct matters. I have talked much with our Lord, and with Jayderay. We will hold service for the children in our way, when we deem it appropriate."

She hugs him quickly, pecks Jayderay on a cheek, and slips back to her Elvis.

Jayderay beams at her almost husband. Women often quit this beaming after a few years of the man being a *real* husband. Once married men often have a brief shelf life.

"She fine with this, RL. And I'm fine with *everything* since I got you back," she says, slipping her arms around him.

Hugging her back, he says, "Oh, honey, you feel so, just so... right."

That earns him a kiss that was meant to be a quickie. But almost develops into something hardly fitting for a time of burial.

It is true: Absence does make the heart grow fonder. And that magnifies beyond measure when thinking someone is dead... and then finding out they're not. It's like falling in love all over again.

Breaking away, she grins," Okay, enough of that for now, boy. Tell me... what about Frankie?"

RL blows out a breath before saying anything, shaking his head.

"He's still barely speaking, and I don't know what I can do about it. He's being a total horse's ass."

"Honey, that make you and him a even match, you bein' a Donkey Butt most all the time."

"Yeah, and you tell me that most all the time," he chuckles. "But I can't help it I don't know what happened. Really, I DO NOT KNOW."

"RL, I done said I believe you that first time you told us. But you and me know this house better than Frankie do. We spent *hours* looking for him on just the second floor, and never went in the same room twice. And we like to not ever found our way out. This house is fooly."

"But he oughta know that by now," RL says, sighing. "I just flat don't know what to do about this."

"RL, that boy love you. He does with all his heart. It most killed him when you fell."

"I know that... and I... I love him back, I guess," he says blushing.

"Ain't no... there is no *guess* to it RL. You two like father and son and you know it. And he do too. Now, you listen to me; this fuss is temporary; it's only drift away stuff. You just let it alone."

RL nods. He will follow this advice.

Heeding advice is good practice for a man about to be married.

Men need lots of advice.

Especially married ones.

Back at the grave, RL tells Frankie what the two women have decided. He's hoping this will open some kind of dialogue.

Hoping is about all it is. Frankie simply nods silently, and starts filling the grave.

With another sigh, RL picks up his spade and joins in.

By unspoken agreement, neither man throws or tosses dirt into the opening. They lower each shovel full in, and gently empty it.

Occasionally, one will kneel, patting and pressing the loose soil by hand.

The filling is finished much too soon; magnifying how pitiful and small the grave is. There was so achingly little to bury of three children.

Silently putting the shovels aside, they drop to their knees, raking, smoothing and flattening, using only palms and fingers.

Both men stay at this much longer than necessary. Much longer. They do not speak.

Abruptly Frankie stands, brushing dirt from his hands and knees.

"I'm going to town to buy a doll for them. A big one. I bet they never had a doll."

"No, don't go buy one," says RL. "We don't want to give them any plastic crap. Get three from the shop. The best we have. Those at the shop will be from an older, more age-appropriate time. The girls will like that better."

Frankie nods slowly, saying, "That's a good idea." And he leaves.

Burials should be private, quiet, and attended by those who truly care.

These three little girls had RL and Frankie.

They knew.

And went to sleep.

CHAPTER 23

THE CURTAIN

The Roaton house is not cleansed. It never will be. That is not possible. Nor does it wish to be.

It is however, a quiet home. For now. Its wrapping of dark green vines tends to shield it from the world. The world should be grateful. There are things beneath this house the world could not survive.

Pulled into the barn, and covered with a tarp, sits a garish Cadillac hearse. Its owner will not ever need it again. He no longer can drive. But he's around. Both Jayderay and RL are worried that Frankie might get to thinking about this vehicle.

And get up to something. He's known for that.

Inside the house, that secret panel is still open. No one knows how to close the sneaky, clever bastard. But nobody bothers to go back up to the attic anyway. The girl ghosts have gone. Shadow has affirmed that. And there can be no better authority.

Up those once hidden steps, the rooms are no longer cold. Those three doors stand wide open now. All is still swirled with dust and cobwebs, but the flooring is sound, solid and true. There are no dangers of anyone falling through.

Or anything coming out.

One room has a huge drawing on the floor. It seems crudely executed, as if by children.

It's of a web. A web drawn in chalk.

And that huge, rusty, banded iron chest still sits in this attic, forgotten.

Noises come from it.

The sound of living meat.

Some things will not stay forgotten.

━━━ ✦ ✦ ━━━

In the Waydowns, fogs drift, abandoned work stations blink, animals scream, live and die. And on it goes. As it has for decades.

A girl with nappy white hair and pinkish eyes picks her way cautiously along a corridor. Holding a gun that she doesn't know anything about... except how to pull the trigger. Usually, that's quite enough.

She spots a familiar looking hatch, closed and locked. This will help in locating her lab coat. She needs that coat, she plans on some fishing in her future.

Nearing the door, she hears an enraged Eeed chittering furiously and pounding its head against the metal. Good, this is the right hatch.

Sure enough, not too far away, she finds the coat. Ripped but intact, and definitely fit for angling.

And on she goes, wearing it. She's lonely. She misses her home. It has water from the wall. Her Da had found it.

Through the constantly drifting haze, she sees a Lab Spill far ahead.

It's scared, bewildered and lost, as most are.

The girl watches the sad creature for a while.

Her crooked mouth twitches, almost smiles. She pockets the gun.

But she keeps her hand on it.

———•◆•———

Also, in the Waydowns, not very far away from the girl:

Doctor Moto is very much alive, as he will be for many decades. And he's very much aware. And he's wishing. He's wishing that he had stayed inside that boulder. Or was up a dinosaur's butt.

Very, very, very far away from everything, Moses is talking to Commander SON.

"Keep yourself handy, Junior. I'm about to deliver the earth reports. They never go over very well. So I may need you to help me with HIM."

"Earth!" snorts the commander with disgust. "Those eternal pains. Why don't we do something about that wretched hive?"

Moses stares. "Seems to me you were sent down to do just that, not too many centuries ago. And what a right proper cockup you made of that."

"Well, well, well... humans are just, just impossible!" splutters the commander.

"Indeed. That Magdalene girl you got to fiddlin' around with was quite *possible*."

The commander coughs. "That was just a misunderstanding."

"Yes," says Moses, his bushy eyebrows arching. "And they're still *misunderstanding* it down there to this very day. Anyway, quit twisting your toga up into your privates, I don't give a Sunday School Psalm about that crap. You just wait here."

He quietly enters the Sanctified Chambers, where Gregorian chants play in the background. Softly laying a scroll on the desk... he gets the hell out of there.

Presently, God picks it up, feeds it into the reader. Within less than a minute, he shouts, "WHAT!" and promptly collapses, white hair splaying out over the marble top.

In the antechamber, Moses stands at a monitor screen watching. He nods knowingly, turns to SON, saying, "Told you. Earth news does it every time. Help me get him to his cloud."

In town, there are benefits being derived from previous actions by Frankie:

An exceedingly unhappy orthodontist sits in his attorney's office. He's being sued by an even unhappier patient. For much more than simply a lot of money. The amount could empty a bank.

It seems a drug addict old woman had been found in the tooth-yanker's parking lot which caused total pandemonium in his reception area.

The patient, who had nothing whatsoever to do with the druggie, was forgotten. Behind a closed door, he'd been left clamped in a chair, mouth yawning to the heavens. He was forgotten for a very, very long time.

He still cannot shut his mouth. Maybe not ever.

Nor is this the only trouble the miserable orthodontist is having.

His receptionist, whom he had called a cow during that stressful time in the office, is also unhappy. Expensively so.

She, being a Vassar graduate, would not be treated in such a cavalier manner. She's quitting.

AND, she has informed him, she is just a little bit preggers, and if proper emolument was not forthcoming, quickly and a lot, the orthodontist's loving wife would be told... quickly and a lot.

The dentist is in imminent, certain danger of having to fork over huge amounts of cash. He will weep. Copiously.

He'd much rather be forking over something he wouldn't mind parting with. Like his children.

Dentists have a reputation for being mighty hunters. Some are known to spend exorbitant sums to go on safaris. On these hunting expeditions, they have the delight of bravely shooting incredibly dangerous, caged lions. Sometimes with arrows.

The hunter is positive this makes his penis grow larger. This is something all hunters need.

Their wives would agree. Heartily agree.

Yes, this particular dentist/orthodontist/tooth yanker is a hunter. And quite proud of it. As proof of his manhood, he has mounted heads tastefully arrayed on the walls of his opulent home.

Good for him. Let his financial fornication commence, and his squalling begin.

The animals will weep. Copiously.

———— ◆◆◆ ————

Frankie benefit # 2:

In one of the local hospitals, a drug addict old woman drifts in and out of consciousness. She's been medicated to sleep a lot. The nurses see to this with great zeal, as the old woman is... a ferocious bitch.

Found unconscious in some dentist's parking lot, she had been admitted with knots on her head. And absolutely raving about what she was going to do.

She ranted to the doctor about a "cheating faggot, cock-sucking queer, homo mother fucker" that had robbed her. And that she was going to "shoot his perverted depraved ass off, and all fudge packers should be hung," and on she raged. And on.

The doctor was gay. He quietly listened. And immediately prescribed sedatives. In large and frequent doses. The nurses were eager to administer the medication.

He quickly contacted the harridan's daughter with his recommendation of having this woman declared, non-compos mentos. In simple terms: she's a fruitcake, with termites in her tower, and can't take care of herself. He also mentions the phrase, in loco parentis, to the daughter.

The daughter agrees heartily. She will sacrifice all her life plans, and take over the mother's affairs.

Someone can always be found to take over the affairs of a relative... providing the dear, sainted, beloved relative... has money.

If not: pitch'em in a ditch.

The caring daughter now drive's about in mom's new Mercedes. Taking care of those affairs.

———◆◆◆———

In town, RL and Jayderay sit beneath the towering Pecan trees, sipping iced tea, and listening to the raucous choir of cicadas. And discussing the hiring of a moving company.

She wants to. He does not. This means they will.

This is the only sure way to a happy marriage... do what the wife wants. She's the smart one. And regardless of brain size, if the man has any survival skills, he will... do what the wife wants.

Princess is laying in the grass between them, tongue lolling out, wearing the huge grin dog's do so well.

When her two humans had arrived back from the Roaton house, Princess had been overjoyed as always. And she had given RL an even more thorough licking than usual. Plus, a particularly serious vacuuming with her big nose.

The dog knows something happened to this man. She had heard him scream. But obviously RL is RL. Maybe not exactly the same, but he passed the nose test. Which is quite a big deal.

George, being a cat, was not quite so effusive in his welcome. He did wake, opened yellow eyes, and purred as RL petted. George knows it's not good for RL to feel too loved. He might become spoiled, and that can't be tolerated. Being spoiled is a cat's province. Looking at his human through half lidded eyes, the cat thinks.

...Fell down into neverland didn't you? I heard you scream... you turnip. How you manage to survive when you're away from me is beyond comprehension.

And now, about this moving crap... how about you just bring me back a tee shirt?

———— ◆◆◆ ————

RL and Jayderay, having settled the moving company issue so easily, move on to other things. Of huge importance is Shadow and Elvis.

"RL, he ain't gettin' no... he's not getting any better. How can we possibly help a... a... a whatever he is? And Shadow refuse to see it, she just smile and talk about prayin' him well. My Gramma always said, new Christians was new fools. Pray him well! Funeral homes just love that kinda talk. RL, I think... I really do think that boy might die."

"No, that won't happen," he says with feeling. "Will not happen. We still have that breastplate-portal thing. I went through it once before to kidnap a ship's doctor for him; I'll do it again."

"Yeah, you and Frankie did... and drug back that awful Moto man. I most forgot about that breastplate devilness... No, let's don't think about doin' that unless there's no other—"

"Jayderay! RL interrupts, sitting up straight, sloshing his tea, eyes going wide. He just realized he's forgotten something. And it's never good to forget about things in the Roaton house. They will come for you... in the night.

"Honey, what... what's in that iron chest?"

THE END

Want more of the Roaton house... and beneath? Then read the other eruptions:

THE COOL THING
LAB SPILL
THE WAYDOWNS,
and coming soon:

RANCID RAINBOW

Lush praise, constructive criticism... or constipated complaints, can be directed to:

Rife6000@aol.com

And thanks for reading! Robert Rife

PRAISE FOR THE BOOKS
by Robert Rife

"... fun, frightening, and ribald. ***It won't be for everybody, but that can be said of all great writing.***"

"... delightfully weird... this story will blow you away!"

"Original, impressive, compulsively entertaining..."

"... scary and frequently hilarious..."

"The Cool Thing is gloriously twisted, and scared the s**it out of me!"

"... blows the genre out of the water..."

———— ✦ ✦ ✦ ————

"Stephen King meets Terry Pratchett... funny and terrifying..."

———— ✦ ✦ ✦ ————

"...action-rich... visceral imagery and heart-stopping horror..."

———— ✦ ✦ ✦ ————

"...irreverent and darkly funny. Injecting brutal scenes with almost lyrical prose lends the novel a definite otherworldly feel."

———— ✦ ✦ ✦ ————

"Lures the reader in fast, Cool Thing delivers!

———— ✦ ✦ ✦ ————

"A bold, unconventional gem!"

———— ✦ ✦ ✦ ————

"...vivid near cinematic imagery with pacing that never slows down."

"I have never read anything like this. Lab Spill is fabulous."

"Best sci-fi all year!"

"Roller coaster fast, weirdly original, and delightfully believable..."

"Wicked awesome!"

"Laughs, scares, and tears... written with much heart..."

"What a series! The Waydowns needs to be a movie!"

———◆◆◆———

"If you like King, you will LOVE this."

———◆◆◆———

"... the story moves faster than a UFO."

———◆◆◆———